A BRIDE FOR TWO BILLIONAIRES

The Male Order, Texas Collection

Lola Newmar

MENAGE EVERLASTING

Siren Publishing, Inc.
www.SirenPublishing.com

A SIREN PUBLISHING BOOK
IMPRINT: Ménage Everlasting

A BRIDE FOR TWO BILLIONIARES
Copyright © 2011 by Lola Newmar

ISBN-10: 1-61034-213-5
ISBN-13: 978-1-61034-213-1

First Printing: January 2011

Cover design by *Les Byerley*
All art and logo copyright © 2011 by Siren Publishing, Inc.

ALL RIGHTS RESERVED: This literary work may not be reproduced or transmitted in any form or by any means, including electronic or photographic reproduction, in whole or in part, without express written permission.

All characters and events in this book are fictitious. Any resemblance to actual persons living or dead is strictly coincidental.

Printed in the U.S.A.

PUBLISHER
Siren Publishing, Inc.
www.SirenPublishing.com

A BRIDE FOR TWO BILLIONIARES

The Male Order, Texas Collection

LOLA NEWMAR
Copyright © 2011

Prologue

Taylor Ewing inhaled deeply as she came upon the vibrant blankets of bluebonnets along the empty interstate. The aroma of the blooms and the freshly cut grass enveloped her senses as she passed a gigantic, green row-crop tractor slaving in the cotton field off in the distance to her right. The clean country air and summer warmth that caressed her skin eased the tension in her aching muscles. There was just something about Texas summer that trivialized troubles.

And Taylor had her share of troubles.

The over-packed vintage hat boxes and Louis trunks surrounding her at least served as comforting reminders that she did not need to worry any longer. With every faded green exit sign that passed, Taylor cruised closer to Male Order and farther from Dallas. Farther from the high rises of the glittering downtown, farther from the stumbling, drunk beauties carrying roofie coladas, farther from the hairsprayed, bedazzled pageant scene, and farther from the pain of knowing most of her twenty-four years were spent trying to satisfy plastic friends and bored, image-conscious parents.

The life-changing event of two weeks ago swam through her conscience like a relentless man-eating shark. She had arrived home late after a grueling twelve-hour day at her step-father's public relations firm where she had apprenticed for the past couple of years since graduating from state. She remembered tossing her black stilettos under the small table by the door before walking through the apartment she shared with Dillon.

Dillon Day, lead singer of Daybed, was an up-and-coming rock star out of Austin, and Taylor had been dating him for about ten months, instantly making them both paparazzi favorites within the precocious Dallas social scene. Within hours of their initial meeting, relationship buzz surrounding the rock star and the southern pageant queen was all over Emilio Estefan's infamous Dallas society gossip blog, Allegedly.com, sealing their fate as the newest it-couple of the city.

As Taylor made her way to her bedroom door, she had come to a sudden, startled halt right as she began to twist the door knob.

"Oh, Bobby! Stuff my cunt with that big cock! Fuck me stupid, Daddy!"

What the—Amber and Bobby? Taylor could hear the gross, wet slapping of sweaty, naked skin accompanying the voices of her long-time friend, Amber, and Dillon's drummer, Bobby Smalls.

Then there was a third voice, a familiar voice, a voice that made her heart drop to her sore feet. "C'mon, you filthy little whore. Don't stop sucking my cock! And don't act like my balls aren't there, either, bitch."

Oh my God! Dillon!

When she had swung open the door, her jaw nearly dropped to the floor. She would never forget the devious grin on Amber's overly-made-up face as she looked back over her shoulder to an awe-struck Taylor, keeping her position on all fours between the two band mates.

Taylor had stood there astonished, watching Dillon mutter a string of excuses, using only his mesh Ed Hardy trucker hat to cover his crotch as Amber moved to the corner in a giggling fit, not bothering to cover up her bony, nude, fake-baked body.

"I swear on my mama, Taylor, she just sucked my dick. It was a—a—an accident! Yeah, yeah, that's what happened, an accident!"

Slow to comprehend the situation, likely from an overabundance of his hourly herbal refreshments, Bobby finally glanced around, his bare ass still facing the bedroom door. He smiled under half-closed, stoned eyes when he spotted Taylor. "Oh, shit! Hey, Taylor! I didn't even see you back there, man." He gave her a sloppy wave with one hand as he took a puff of his fat joint with the other.

Amber had been a close friend for over ten years since she and Taylor met at the Miss Teen Dallas Texas Yellow Rose conference as tweens. Amber's father was an important client of Harold's, Taylor's eclectic step-father. They had introduced the girls, and it only seemed natural when Amber invited Taylor into her clique of other over-privileged, label-lusting, gorgeous young girls.

But as she stood in the doorway, her friend, boyfriend, and boyfriend's drummer all scattered around the room in a nude chaos, Taylor didn't feel heartbroken. She just felt exhausted.

The next morning, she told her mother she would be taking up Aunt Veronica's offer to come stay with her in her small town, just to clear her head and evaluate what she wanted once she returned home. Aunt Veronica was the only living relative on Taylor's father's side, and they had kept in close touch since his death. Her mother didn't particularly like the idea of her "sophisticated daughter" living with her wild-child sister-in-law, but Taylor wasn't asking for permission, only informing her mother of where she would be for the next month.

Now, it was literally all behind her.

As the Texas summer breeze hummed around her, Taylor silently thanked her mother's husband for buying her the adorable convertible Beetle instead of the hardtop. Harold had insisted on the going-away gift. She opted for the beige exterior with the peanut butter top and peanut butter interior. Although she was wearing her favorite white Chanel sunglasses with extra buggy lens, the sun was shining bright enough to make her slightly squint against the harsh afternoon sun as she cruised east on Interstate 25.

As "The Boys of Summer" began to play on the radio, Taylor turned up the volume and set her focus on the twelve miles she had left until she reached Male Order, Texas.

Chapter 1

Brody Bartlett lifted his hands from his mother's eyes to reveal her latest birthday gift. He heard her gasp with delight as he walked from behind her to see her reaction.

"She's gorgeous," said Mama. Desire glazed over her crystal blue eyes as she looked over the perfectly curvy form before her, then she looked over at her son. "Did you really buy her for *me?*"

"She's all yours, Mama. You deserve it." Brody grabbed his mother's hand and led her over to the sleek grand touring car parked in her driveway, a blue Bugatti Veyron just hours off the lot. He opened the door and helped her in. "This is the Bleu Centenaire, one of the special editions. Most Veyrons are two-toned, but the monotone on this one makes it look sharp."

Mama settled into the ivory leather seats and slowly ran her palms along the thick, ivory steering wheel. "Baby, this is too much. You know I don't need a two million dollar car. I only drive long distances when I want to make my shopping trips to Dallas—"

"Which you make every weekend," Brody interrupted. Mama released a heavy sigh in response to his stubbornness, shaking her head as she looked over the fine detailing of the interior.

Although she performed her best attempt at modesty, Brody knew his mother much too well. Mama and modesty were like oil and water. No matter how hard she might try, they just didn't mix. This was a woman who had a closet that housed so many shoes and jewelry it made Imelda Marcos's closet look like a vacant medicine cabinet.

But he knew how to convince her. "Besides, I've yet to tell you the best part about this fine automobile."

Mama looked up at him, one inquisitive brow lifting in obvious curiosity. "Oh?"

"It goes from zero to a hundred in two-point-five seconds and tops off at two-seventy." Just as he expected, her baby blues widened in amazement then again danced around the car in newfound fascination. Besides her family, there were only two other things he knew that made his mother's heart skip a beat—a limo full of shopping bags after a day-long shopping trip and a car that could drive so fast you'd swear your guts were begging for salvation.

"Well," she drew out, obvious guilt forming in her features, "all right, I accept."

Brody smiled wide, bent down, and gave Mama a kiss on the cheek.

"Take it as a token of appreciation for the last twenty-nine years. I can always count on you for anything, and you never pass judgment. You're a good woman, Mama, and you're the food to my soul."

Mama climbed out of the car and embraced him in a tight hug. She released him, and he could see the tears of joy forming in her eyes. "Your words sure have a way of convincing a girl, baby, but the only thank you I need is you. I've raised a caring, successful young man, a billionaire in his own right, and that's my reward." Brody smiled and hugged her once again. "Where's your partner in crime?"

"Jay is inside arguing with Bradley over taking his bags to his room. You know how he insists on doing everything himself." His best friend and business partner, Jay Stephens, had always expressed his apprehension at taking advantage of their family butler. *Take a break, Bradley. I'm perfectly capable of doing it myself,* he'd always say.

"So what are your plans for the day, Mama?"

"Well, I'm expected at the city hall in an hour. We just have a few loose ends to tie before the cotillion next week. Your fathers flew to

London yesterday on business, and they won't be back until the day before the ball." Papa Kendrick was a few years older than his brother, Papa Derek, and usually served as the Bartlett family representative at the town meetings. But with both of Brody's fathers in the international transportation industry, it meant Mama had to step in to oversee their duties when they were away. "Have you and Jay decided which lucky girl will be your date? For the past eleven months, every eligible bachelorette in Male Order, and beyond, has been pestering me about your decision this year."

"No, not yet. I'm not sure what's gotten into Jay lately, but he's worrying me. He used to love picking a date for the cotillion. He looked forward to it. But this year, he just gets all pissy when I bring it up. He keeps saying he's too busy to worry about 'some petty dance.'" Brody leaned against the car and crossed his arms in front of his chest as a small fire of frustration lit within. "Mama, I think he's changed his mind."

"About what, darlin'?" she asked as she continued to inspect the car, her attention still focused on her birthday present.

"I don't think he wants a family with me anymore." Just speaking his fears aloud caused Brody's stomach to clench in a panic.

Mama quickly turned to face him. "That's ridiculous," she snapped in disbelief. "Jay cares about you more than anything in this world. You both know firsthand how wonderful a ménage family can be."

"Yeah? Then tell me why he didn't even think to invite me along with the last three girls he went out with."

Mama's brow burrowed with confusion. "There must be some explanation." Brody could see the disappointment crossing his mother's face. He knew his mother had grown to love Jay like her own, and she wanted nothing more than for the Stephenses and the Bartletts to join together as one family.

It was no secret Brody had always planned to share a wife and children with Jay. Although either had yet to fall in love with a woman, Brody always had faith it would happen one day, when it was right. Now it seemed that dream was slipping right through his fingers.

* * * *

Jay closed the front door behind him and walked down the long, wide steps of the Bartlett mansion. Down the driveway, he could see Mrs. Bartlett holding Brody's hands in front of her while she talked to him. Jay couldn't hear what they were saying, but he knew from Brody's expression he was upset about something. It hurt him to see his best friend upset, but lately Jay was not one to lift anyone's spirits.

He looked around at the fifteen-acre estate, scanning the area for any change that might have taken place since their visit last summer. The impeccable, short-cut grass, the perfectly trimmed shrubbery, the long, winding cobblestone driveway was all just as he remembered. The Bartletts had been one of the five founding families of Male Order. Brody's parents still lived in the original Bartlett house, the biggest mansion on the west side of town.

Jay looked down at his watch. They had been in Male Order for exactly thirteen minutes, giving his mother more than enough of time to get word of their arrival.

"Jay-Jay!"

And surprise, surprise, there she was, already jogging his way, joy-filled tears in her eyes. She held her floppy, white straw hat down with her left hand as it threatened to run away with the greedy breeze. She used her other hand to slightly lift her long, yellow sundress away from the inefficient sky-high wedge sandals that limited her speed.

"Craig, come quick! Our baby is home!" Jay instantly felt a warm blanket of familiarity wrap over him as his mother swung her arms around his waist and dug her head in his chest. "Oh, my baby, my baby!"

Jay let out a long laugh as he placed his hands on her small shoulders. "Mom, I'm thirty years old. That's hardly a baby."

"Oh, Jay. Always talking nonsense," she retorted in her heavy country drawl. She then turned toward his father who was still making his way from their classic teal '67 Ferrari GT S/4. Their house wasn't far down the street, so Jay figured his parents must've heard from the neighbors that they were riding through town. Word traveled at the speed of light in Male Order. "Craig, dear, we arrived just in time to catch Jay and Brody pull up." Motherly pride was apparent in her voice as she held Jay's arm tight in hers.

"Hi, Pops."

Pops took off his thick, black-rimmed glasses to quickly clean them with his tailored button-down shirt, whistling as he put them back on his face. "Well, well, nice ride ya'll got Lucy there, boy. She's sure to look ravishing behind the wheel."

"Don't even think about it, old man." They all turned toward Brody's cheerful voice as he made his way across the vast lawn with his mother on one arm. Brody's mood seemed to lift as he walked over to Pops and bent down to give him a hug.

"Aw, Mr. Stephens, I believe you've grown since I last saw you," Brody teased.

"You little shit!" Pops playfully nudged Brody away from him as they all laughed.

"Isn't it great to have our boys back?" Mrs. Bartlett hugged Brody close. Her long, wavy brown hair framed her naturally beautiful, heart-shaped face, and it always looked intentionally wild and beachy, a striking contrast to the extravagant jewelry that was widely known to be her signature. The tears in Mrs. Bartlett's crystal blue eyes pooled above her bottom lashes as she rubbed Brody's stomach with her left hand, her right arm around his waist. Although Mrs. Bartlett was tall for a woman at five foot nine, her son still managed to dwarf her when she stood next to him. "It's nice to see you finally take a break from that Yellow Rope to actually come visit your families."

"It's The *Velvet* Rope, Mama," Brody corrected. "The Yellow Rope sounds like a network for serial killers."

"Well, whatever you call it. All I know is it has stolen my son away from me for the past decade, and I'm just grateful when you actually find time for me. Thank the heavens you finally sold it. It was taking up too much of your time. You worked so hard on that business, and you two deserve some rest and relaxation along with a homemade meal and a good night's sleep."

Jay knew Mrs. Bartlett was right. His and Brody's lives had been fiercely dominated by the time and work it took to run The Velvet Rope since they started the social networking Web site when they were freshman at Stanford.

When the two young men first moved to California, they were immediately pulled into the Golden State's energetic, non-stop party scene. After only a few short weeks of living there, the men realized their little black books just weren't cutting it. It had quickly become complicated to remember the names of their new associates and the details of all the parties happening around town, especially when they still needed time to manage their university work. Both men were in Stanford's honors business program, so the less time they spent trying to organize their invites, the more time they had to be successful students. In an effort to better manage their social calendars, the men had developed the idea for The Velvet Rope.

The Velvet Rope gave each user an online party profile along with a user-friendly, electronic social calendar to organize social events. The user could sign on to their usernames and scan through the thousands of social events posted on the Web site on a daily basis. Some events could be open to the public, or The Velvet Rope member could choose to only invite certain people. The users also had the option to filter the parties by location, college, theme, and even liquor selection. Last year, they'd sold The Velvet Rope to one of the Internet's leading search engines for twelve billion dollars.

"You know, Jay and I were actually thinking about sticking around for a while. Since the company has been bought, we've come to realize how tired we are and how much we miss the simple life. We thought a long vacation here in Male Order, staying in our childhood homes, might give us the rest we need." An outburst of cries of excitement and hugs surrounded the men as their parents took turns embracing each of them.

"So how about some lunch?" asked Jay once their parents caught their breaths. "We could all head to Hester's Steakhouse. I could use a juicy Kobe burger topped with some shiitake mushrooms." He felt his stomach roar its agreement.

"I don't think so, young man," said Mom, her finger waving in his face as she scolded him. "No son of mine is coming home just to have a *burger*. We can all come back to the house, put some ribs on the grill, and I'll prepare some mustard potato salad and collard greens with salt pork. There's an '82 Chateau Margaux I'm dying to open, anyway." Brody was as welcomed in the Stephens' home as Jay was, and vice-versa. Jay always took comfort in knowing how much love their families had for each other.

"Oh, Mrs. Stephens, you're the best." Brody sweetly hugged her as she giggled. "And you know I have to have some of that famous sweet sun tea you make. No one makes it as sweet as you do." Brody winked, and Mom visibly blushed and giggled, obviously flattered.

"I would be delighted to join you, but the town meeting will be starting soon," said Mrs. Bartlett as she observed the time on her extra large diamond watch. Brody's fathers always made sure Mrs. Bartlett's jewelry fetish was fulfilled, and this was no doubt their latest indulgence. But as beautiful as she was, she was not a typical trophy wife, for Mrs. Bartlett's charm and incredible intelligence always served Male Order well. "But you boys go on ahead. A home-cooked meal would do you plenty good. Thanks for feeding my boy, Julie."

"*Our* boys, Lucy," Mom corrected with a wink.

* * * *

"Oh, I almost forgot!" exclaimed Papa Craig. He turned from his ten-foot-wide barbecue toward Brody and Jay as he opened another bottle of Shincr. "Guess what I bought your cousins." His face twitched as he struggled to maintain his composure, but he looked like he would burst with excitement at any moment.

Before they were even given the chance to guess, Jay heard two loud engines behind him. Seconds later his twin cousins, eighteen-year-old Grayson and Gavin, rounded the corner of the house in matching lime-green GG Quad four-wheelers.

"They run about fifty a piece, but I got both of them for ninety," Papa Craig stated proudly. Most wealthy men bragged about how much money they spent, but being new money, Papa Craig always bragged about the bargains he found.

"Grand!" exclaimed Mom with a roll of her eyes. "Ninety thousand dollars for a couple of *go-karts*."

"They're four-wheelers, dear, and they're top of the line. I closed a big deal last week, and I wanted to celebrate with the family. I just consider it an early graduation present for my nephews." Papa shrugged casually.

Grayson and Gavin took off their helmets as they came to a stop in front of their family. The teenaged twins simultaneously shook dark curls out of identical faces and gave their audience identical, cocky smiles. Everything about the boys, from their chiseled cheekbones to their bow-legged walks, was identical, except Grayson's eyes were a sage green and Gavin's were a blue topaz.

Jay could feel a smile threatening at the sight of his "little" cousins, swiftly looking more like men every summer. He guessed they must have grown a good four inches since last summer, and their boyish features were starting to show maturity in their strong jaw lines and towering forms. The twins had lived with the Stephenses since they were taken in at three years old. Their mother was a barfly-alcoholic that gave her rights up as their mother to her brother, Craig. It seemed like raising two boys took too much time away from her honky-tonks and her search for Mr. Right Now. Jay's parents didn't hesitate to take the twin boys into their arms and their homes, and they had continued to treat Grayson and Gavin as their own. Jay's relationship with his cousins had quickly grown deeper over the years, more into that of a big brother.

"Ha! Nice shoes, ladies," teased Grayson, giving them a mocking smirk. Jay and Brody looked down at the John Varvatos leather oxfords that were sent to them last year for the Sundance Film Festival, then they looked up and shot glares at the twins.

"Get off, Mary Kate and Ashley," Brody demanded, raising his fist in warning. "It's our turn."

"Psh! Not on your life, woman."

"Now!" growled Jay. His cousins were off the vehicles before he could make a complete step in their direction.

Sandbox domination never dies.

* * * *

The warm sun shone through the canopy of trees in Aunt Veronica's backyard, putting a spotlight on Taylor's body and giving her the perfect light as she painted her toenails with the cherry red polish she picked up at Aurora's beauty shop down the street. She worked carefully as the summer heat caressed her freshly lotioned skin.

Since moving to Male Order a week ago, she had taken advantage of Aunt Veronica's lawn chairs to lie out every afternoon and now had a healthy, bronze glow to her body. She had just gone downtown earlier that week to buy a vintage bikini, yellow with white polka dots and a balconette top that gave the perfect support for her ample breasts.

Taylor knew in her gut Male Order would be the perfect, small Texas town. Although it was a town built in luxury, it was welcoming, cozy, and everyone waved to her as she walked down the street as though they had known her for years. It was only a half hour down the road from Dallas, yet Male Order seemed like another planet.

With her nearest charity event a full three weeks away, she lay back and inhaled the town's positive energy as she reveled in knowing she had no obligations for the rest of her mini-vacation. Before she had come outside, she had made a quick phone call to her hypertrophic cardiomyopathy charity headquarters for any schedule updates she would be facing once she headed back after her month-long hiatus. She had then marked reminders on her calendar for an upcoming art auction and the eleventh annual, and no doubt successful, HCM middle school tour for heart disease awareness.

Taylor hadn't understood her mother's apprehension toward the Male Order trip, for Taylor had never been one to listen to idle gossip. She assumed what she heard about the small Texas town was just a bunch of exaggeration. Rumor was the town had been founded by ten wealthy men who ordered ten mail order brides, but by mistake, they were only sent five. In order to preserve their investment, the men all shared a wife. But then Veronica told her Male Order *was* a ménage town. By town tradition, every female resident was entitled to have a committed relationship with however many men she fell in love with. Most of the women had two lovers, but Taylor had once seen a woman with *five* husbands at the Male Order diner.

This was all so new to Taylor. Although she always had the firm belief that people should have the right to love freely, she couldn't deny that the idea of a ménage lifestyle had initially taken her aback. She had been raised by a conservative mother whose every action was made in attempt to catapult her status another step up the Dallas social ladder.

When Taylor was twelve, her father had died suddenly from HCM. A hardworking, dedicated man who'd worked in construction since he was fifteen, no one suspected he was sick. The congenital heart disease did what it was known to do best, and it took Taylor's daddy away without a hint of warning. And no one missed him more than Taylor. She could still remember standing at their front door at 5:22 every afternoon as a child as she waited for her daddy to pull up to the driveway in his white work truck.

When her father died, Taylor's mother had been forced to work two jobs to support the suddenly single-parent household. Taylor remembered how her mother would leave at 6 A.M. and return home at 9 P.M. Taylor had quickly learned to take care of herself while her mother was away. She always hoped her newfound independence would be a sort of payment to her mother for all the hard work she did to support the household of two.

A year later, her mother got a gig to clean houses in the rich Dallas suburbs. After one random night out cleaning a mansion for an unusually long ten hours, Taylor's mother came rushing in Taylor's bedroom, completely decked out in a French maid costume that looked like it belonged at a cheesy sorority Halloween party.

"Mama, what the—"

"Baby, it's over. It's all over, baby girl. All our worries are *over*." With mascara streaming down her face in black tears, Taylor's mother held her close as she sobbed on her daughter's shoulder.

A month later, her mother married Harold King IV, a fifty-five-year-old trust-fund baby and third generation CEO of King Public Relations and Marketing, the leading PR company in Dallas for the past fifty years.

Harold was an odd gentleman. Although many considered him a kind man, he was known more for his partying than his business sense. Growing up with a silver spoon in his mouth, Harold never had to have any. He had money to hire other people for all that.

There was always a cabernet glass glued to his right hand, and he would make erratic spasms he called dance moves as he moved to the silent beat constantly playing in his head. When he wasn't singing or dancing horribly, he was usually tripping over something.

While her father had been charming and poised, Harold was clumsy and awkward. He might not have been Taylor's first choice for her mother, but she knew Harold was dedicated to making her mother happy, and she was thankful for that.

Suddenly, she heard a duet of singing voices thick with country-grammar flavor. The harmony broke through Taylor's intense concentration. Her gaze followed the sound over to one of the neighbor's backyards.

Over the picket fence, she could see an old woman in a wheelchair sitting on her back porch. Her hands rested on a white cane standing between her feet as she smiled lovingly at the two old men sitting on either side of her. She softly swayed to the beat as her two husbands each strummed a ukulele and sang her an old Texas tune in rich harmony. Taylor's heart clenched with emotion and fascination at the sight of the happy old trio.

Being loved by two men! I can't imagine.

* * * *

Brody sped by the lush, emerald yards as he tailed Jay in the four-wheelers. Jay was more reckless than Brody, randomly flying over the street curb, his four-wheeler always landing on the right two wheels as it threatened to tip over. But each time, Jay would manage to speed off into the neighborhood even faster.

"You're going to kill yourself, Johnny Knoxville!" Brody called out, but Jay just flashed him a crooked grin over his shoulder, not slowing down a bit. Brody couldn't help but smile back at his longtime best friend.

This reminded Brody of the beginning of it all. The days of riding their dirt bikes through the fields of Male Order, using Lone Star beer cans for shooting practice, and jumping in the lake in their school uniforms from the highest tree they could find were all cherished memories of the carefree childhood they had shared together.

Jay had been his partner in crime since they met in pee-wee football almost twenty-five years ago. Football had transformed them from babies to dedicated athletes. In fact, their chemistry on the field, with Jay as quarterback and Brody as receiver, brought Male Order a few state high school football titles in their day. Their legacies as football heroes and successful billionaire alumni always guaranteed the men an abundance of homemade pies from the local bachelorettes when they came back to Male Order every summer to attend the annual cotillion. Brody's mouth watered at the thought of Stacy Cavallari's spicy-sweet pumpkin and Megan Ray's tart, ripe strawberry.

He suddenly felt a painful tightening in his chest when he remembered the conversation he had with Mama earlier. After all these years together, all the successes and the memories and the promises, Brody just couldn't believe Jay no longer planned to share a ménage lifestyle with him. They were both raised in households with two fathers and one mother, and Brody knew they had both been blessed with happy, fulfilling childhoods.

Since the night they shared their first kiss with Megan Ray during a game of Seven Minutes in Heaven, sharing had always felt natural for Brody. He knew Jay felt the same after their first ménage in college. After that, Jay had rarely brought a woman home without insisting that Brody join in, and with Brody it was the same. When a ménage à trois didn't happen, it was only because one was out of town or too exhausted from long hours in the office.

But Brody wouldn't think about that now. He once again shook his fears from his mind and focused on the small, yet lavish, town around him. As Brody and Jay sped through the neighborhood streets, they began to pass by several familiar yards. Mrs. Cavallari still had the lushest bed of yellow roses in town, the Rays had installed a new pool, and the Jones brothers had built an enormous cherry wood gazebo for their new bride.

Then they passed Miss Veronica Ewing's yard. Brody held his breath. And the world stopped.

He barely heard the mockingbirds singing, or the applause from the nearby little league field, or the lawnmower humming in the next yard over.

There was just *her*.

Her eyes were hidden by oversized, white shades, and her dark auburn hair cascaded down one tan shoulder, her wispy bangs reaching the tops of her perfectly arched eyebrows. As she bent over in the white lawn chair to continue painting her toe nails, the round tops of her breasts pressed against her thighs, pushing the mounds of gold flesh together and daring him to take a bite. The color of her bikini brought out the deep tan of her skin, and he could feel his cock stand to attention at the sight of the healthy glow she radiated.

When she looked up at him and lifted her sunglasses, his breath caught in the back of his throat. With those doe-like, round brown eyes, those heart-shaped lips, she was a vision right out of a pin-up calendar. A beauty mark was just above the right of her upper lip. He imagined it was God's own signature after all the extra time he must have spent on her.

Her eyes started to twinkle as she looked over Brody's body and tossed him the sweetest, most radiant smile he had ever seen in his entire life.

There she is. Finally.

"Brody! Watch out!" He heard Jay's panicked warning from ahead of him just before his four-wheeler ran smack into the street curb, sending Brody flying through the air only to land headfirst into the neighbor's trash can.

Chapter 2

"Real smooth, Brody, real smooth." Jay lifted him out of the hot, rank trashcan by one leg before Brody had the chance to shake the fogginess that flooded his head.

"What the fuck? That damn thing came out of *nowhere*."

"So the street curb came out of nowhere?" Jay laughed as he began removing some of the spaghetti noodles hanging from Brody's head. Brody decided to just ignore his friend's smartass comments.

"Fuck, man, look at all this shit all over me." When Jay didn't reply to his rants, Brody looked up, only to see his best friend transfixed on the life-sized doll that now stood before them with a frightened look on her face, her eyes wide and her lower lip quivering. Brody scanned her petite body. There were no flaws present, only a pair of juicy breasts, flat stomach, and plush hips that tapered down to her tanned thighs. *What a doll.*

She got down on her knees next to Brody, who was now using his elbows to prop himself up as he lay on the ground, his clothes covered in various mystery sauces and gravies. She hesitated a moment then lifted her soft, cool hand to his cheek as she carefully studied his eyes. "Are you all right?" Her voice was that of a sophisticated southern belle, warm and refined.

"I am now." He couldn't keep his eyes from dancing from her shaking lip to the pulse that he could see beating frantically on the left side of her neck. Wow, she really was concerned. And damn, she smelled like Heaven, fresh and light and soft.

Suddenly, a hard, angry look formed on her face, then her gaze darted from Brody to Jay, and back to Brody. "Aren't you two a little *old* to be playing with Big Wheels? You damn near broke your back!"

The brunette Barbie stood up and leaned down to dust the dirt off her knees, allowing Brody to take advantage of the clear view he had of the perfect, succulent feminine orbs that kissed each other in the push-up top holding them in place. He glanced at Jay and saw he took full advantage of the same opportunity.

As she straightened and stood there in the sunlight, her hair created a chestnut-brown halo. *She looks like an angel.* Her soft bangs framed wide, light brown eyes encircled with black fans for eyelashes.

Brody snapped out of his thoughts when ketchup suddenly splattered across his face. Jay had stepped on the half-empty plastic bottle as he scurried to stand in front of the pinup goddess in the yellow bikini. "Damn it, Jay!" Brody used his left shoulder to wipe off the mess on his cheek.

"Afternoon, ma'am. My name is Jay Stephens." Immediately, the angel's faced softened, and her cheeks flushed with color. She reached out for Jay's extended hand as if in a trance over Jay's presence. Even from a distant, Brody noticed the slight shudder in her shoulders when Jay leaned down to kiss the top of her perfectly manicured hand. Then suddenly, she turned her attention to Brody, and she gave him the same killer smile that got him dirty in the first place.

* * * *

Taylor let out a soft laugh as the gorgeous blond stood and let out a small groan. He looked so silly, his designer clothes covered in spaghetti sauce and chocolate pudding and with ketchup splattered on the side of his clean-shaven face.

"I'm Brody Bartlett," he drawled then hissed between his teeth as he started to limp toward her.

"Taylor Ewing. It's a pleasure to meet you, gentleman. I'm staying here with my auntie, Veronica Ewing. I'm here visiting from—" She paused, losing her train of thought when Brody peeled off his stained shirt, revealing a perfectly chiseled torso that belonged on an Olympic swimmer. Taylor swallowed a gasp. "Down from—" Every visible muscle flexed as he worked to wipe away the smears of goo on his gorgeous biceps and inviting neck. There was no stopping the exhale escaping her pursed lips. "Dallas." She quickly looked down at the ground, hoping to hide the heat rising to her face. When she looked up, Brody seemed to be too busy wiping the side his face with the ruined shirt to notice her embarrassment. She was just going to let out a sigh of relief until she looked at Jay. He gave her a little half-smile that let her know he noticed her attraction to Brody. *Damn it.* Taylor quickly returned her gaze to her red toenails until she could feel the heat start to recede.

"Um, are you sure you're okay?" Taylor gathered the courage to look up in their eyes at the risk of revealing her attraction.

"Yes, ma'am, I'm fine. Just a bruised ankle," Brody answered.

There was a long pause as both men's gazes dropped to the cubic zirconia jewelry dangling from her navel, causing Taylor to instinctively cross her arms over her chest.

When she'd woken up this morning, she had thought she was spending the afternoon with only the fluttering monarchs and Jim Morrison's sexy voice to keep her company. The last thing she had expected was for two gorgeous men to come crashing into her life, making her feel self-conscious with their indecent gazes.

Their designer clothes, tailored jeans, and large titanium Nubeo watches reeked of money, wealth, and class despite the simplicity of their casual dress. Most of the wealthy Dallas boys Taylor knew were much gaudier in their fashion choices. But, again, those were just boys. The two fine, dashing specimens standing before her looked far,

far from being boys. Clearing her throat, she lifted her chin to Jay. "Maybe you should be a better babysitter." She hoped the playful jab would divert attention away from her. Both men laughed simultaneously, making Taylor's heart back flip in her chest, and suddenly she was aware of the faint pulse that had moved down to her freshly-shaven pussy lips. Their laughs felt like warm milk and honey, comforting and beautiful and soothing.

"Are you always such a spitfire to complete strangers, Miss Ewing?" asked Jay, wearing an amused smirk on his gorgeous face. His fitted army-green collared shirt brought out the green in his eyes. They were a sparkling contrast paired with his short black hair, perfectly styled even in the Texas humidity. He was a woman's wet dream. He also seemed to be distracted by something on the side of her neck.

When his words registered, she again felt her face flush in shame. She should have been ashamed of herself speaking in such an un-ladylike manner. It seemed that over the last month, she had become a little snappy, not at all her usual warm self. It was as if Dillon built a wall of ice around her heart, and she felt void inside. She was obviously letting her bitterness get the better of her, and despite her promise to not get involved with yet another arrogant spoiled brat, it was no reason for her to be rude.

"My apologies, gentleman. I'm afraid you're right. Excuse my rudeness. It's just been an awfully long month for me."

"Male Order can take some getting adjusted to," added Jay with a quick shrug.

"Oh, it's not the town that bothers me at all." These men were obviously locals, and the last thing she wanted to do was to offend any of the townspeople. "In fact, I've been served heaps of southern hospitality since the day I arrived."

"You can say Male Order citizens have a habit of spoiling their women," Jay said. "As you may have noticed, they tend to get whatever they want."

Taylor knew that was an understatement. Most of the households in Male Order were not only ménage but also extremely wealthy. Judging from the dozens of luxury stores, driveways full of Lamborginis and Bentleys, and blocks and blocks of southern mansions, the citizens of Male Order definitely appreciated the finer things in life.

"Most people with their statuses usually do." Taylor heard the bite in her tone, but she decided to hold back another apology. Sure, the townsfolk were warm and welcoming, but if there was one thing Taylor had learned since Dillon, it was a young, wealthy, handsome man was a wolf in sheep's clothing. Although Dillon had been voted "Sexiest Frontman" by *Texas Monthly*, these two tall glasses of water made her ex look like an unkempt grease monkey. *Stranger danger.*

Jay was just a bit thicker than Brody, and his hair was cut close to his head. As his grin slowly receded, his face again turned serious, and Taylor's mind struggled to relive the image of his smile. She wasn't sure if he knew just how intimidating his clenched jaw and furrowed brow made him look, but she could feel her core twist at the thought of him using that same concentration on her body's most private areas.

Brody, on the other hand, had a sexy, welcoming smile. His friendly face and sun-bleached waves reminded her of the young men that graced the pages of the teen idol magazines she had read as a boy-crazy fifth grader.

She couldn't resist eagerly returning Brody's contagious smile. Taylor realized in embarrassment that it might have been a little too eagerly when Brody let out another soft laugh. She had tried her best to be a lady and not be so obvious, but that had obviously failed.

Brody then shot Jay a knowing look with his chocolate brown eyes before turning them back to a humiliated Taylor. He raked his fingers through his dark gold hair when he finally spoke again. "We apologize for startling you, Miss Ewing, but maybe you'll give us the pleasure of making it up to you."

By instinct, Taylor's eyes narrowed suspiciously on Brody. "What do you mean?"

"Have lunch with us tomorrow." Jay was almost chest to chest with her before Taylor even realized he had taken a step toward her.

She looked up at him, and his intense stare and muscular, warm body were more than enough to make her speechless and left in a hazy fog of lust. Again, the wheels in her head spun in a panic, this time hoping to find an excuse for why she couldn't join them. Taylor needed another egotistical man like she needed a hole in the head. And as gorgeous and charming as these two were, she wouldn't be surprised if their egos needed their own zip codes. "Well, I-I was going to—"

"Look, we don't mean to be rude by the short notice, Miss Ewing, but we promise you won't regret it." At that moment, Taylor realized the southern charm in Brody's voice could make a girl agree to anything he wanted. Taylor could feel her body relax as the Texas Pied Piper's voice melted away her apprehension.

"Call me Taylor, please." She didn't mean for it to come out in a whisper, but she was distracted by Brody, who kept biting his enticing full lips.

"Taylor," Brody repeated softly, letting her name roll off his tongue like smooth honey as he slightly bowed his head in apology and then flashed another grin.

"Your auntie still hanging out at Luscious when the Boom Boom Room is closed?" asked Jay as he used his rough fingers to lightly turn her chin toward him. His warm, unexpected touch sent a wave of sensual tingles down Taylor's body, ending with an ache in her core that caused her pussy to throb in hungry desperation.

"Of course. Almost every day until closing at eight."

"Then we'll meet you there tomorrow, right before lunch." Taylor's pussy clenched unexpectedly at the merely gentle yet swift movement of Jay's thumb over her bottom lip before they turned to walk back to the humming 4 wheelers.

* * * *

"She's the still point of the turning world, Jay. I'm not letting her go." Brody settled in the barber chair, staring at Jay through the mirror in front of him as Mr. Murphy, one of the barbers of the So Fresh Barbershop, flung a black cape around his neck.

Jay sighed heavily in frustration at his best friend's insistence. Brody was diving into this too quick for comfort, and it was getting on Jay's last damn nerve.

"All right, boy, c'mon now. I'm ready for you," Mr. Davis called out to Jay. He beat the previous customer's hair off the now-vacant chair with his towel before throwing it back over his shoulder, where all the barbers at So Fresh kept their towels.

Jay got up from the waiting area against the wall and sat in Mr. Davis's chair. The smell of shaving cream, shampoo, and aftershave was incredibly nostalgic. "C'mon, Brody. Don't be so naïve. She's absolutely gorgeous. I mean, look at her, but you heard your mama after we drove back this afternoon. Taylor's a pageant queen from Dallas. Do you really think she's all that different from any of the L.A. centerfolds we know all too well?"

Brody turned to face Jay's reflection and raised his chin in challenge. "I *know* she's different." Jay rolled his eyes. His friend barely knew the damn woman.

"He has a point, cuz," said Gavin, a few chairs down. "Miss Ewing came to our football practice last week to speak to us about the dangers of HCM. She seemed like an extremely smart woman."

"I was personally disappointed that she didn't show up in her Miss Dallas Texas Yellow Rose crown," said Grayson from another salon chair. "When the other players had asked her why she wasn't wearing it, she said she felt silly wearing a tiara while lecturing about a deadly disease. She had every guy at practice enamored with her. That body!

And, damn, that face. The Lord sure broke the mold with that one. Dillon Day is the biggest dumbass to roam the earth."

"Dillon Day?" Jay thought hard about why that name sounded so familiar.

"Wait," Brody held up a hand, "are you talking about the singer from that band that looks like they never shower?"

"Yeah, Daybed," Grayson replied. "They're nothing but a cheap Ramones rip off with less soap, if you ask me. Anyways, Taylor caught him cheating on her with her *best friend* a few weeks ago. That's why she came to Male Order."

Brody's eyes appeared full of rage as he shook his head in disgust. "That sonuvabitch. He must have a brain of a garden worm for him to hurt a gem like Taylor." Most of the men in the shop nodded and mumbled their agreement at once.

"Gentlemen, gentleman, I'm sure she's an amazing woman, I just can't—"

"You can't what, Jay?" Brody interrupted, sounding more frustrated by the minute. "You can't share a woman with me anymore?"

Jay's heart fell to his feet. He glanced around at the men in the shop, including his cousins, who were now listening intently for his reply. He leaned toward Brody's chair and whispered, "Not here, all right, buddy?"

Mr. Murphy grabbed the sides of Brody's head and forced it back forward. "Now, see, don't you go crying when I fuck up your hair. Now be still." Brody complied but kept his glare on Jay through the reflection in the mirror.

"Stop with the bullshitting, Jay. Taylor Ewing is perfect. She's gorgeous and she's caring and independent. It's obvious your problem lies with me, not her."

"It's not that simple, Brody."

Jay wasn't used to his friend being so stubborn with him. But he could see in Brody's eyes that he honestly thought Taylor was The One.

When Jay heard the loud buzzing of the clippers in Mr. Davis's hand, he was thankful. He hoped it would shut Brody the fuck up, but his nagging friend only called out over the noise, "Like I've always said, Jay, you can lie to yourself, but you can't lie to me."

Growing up, Jay always imagined one day having a marriage like his parents'. His fathers always worked as a team to keep the family happy. There was always a male figure present to attend his games or take him fishing at the lake. If he needed girl advice, he would have the perspectives of two different men to help him through any "life or death" love rut. Most of all, Jay was always forever grateful for the way they made his mother's face light up like a schoolgirl with an obsessive crush every time they walked into the room.

Leaving for college gave Jay an even greater appreciation for Male Order. He had too many West Coast friends who grew up without a father, ignored by their father, or abused by their father. The only thing that held more pain than their lost childhoods was the anger that continued to haunt their souls.

As a boy, Jay had always hoped he would have a wife to share with his best friend one day. The assumption just felt right and natural. But the men were young, and for the last decade, the women he and Brody shared were nothing more than friends or casual encounters. He enjoyed the ménages with Brody. It had even gotten to the point where neither man was thoroughly satisfied unless they shared.

But the cold feet had begun three months ago, right after his thirtieth birthday. Thirty may still be a very young age for a man, but something changed inside him on that day. His wild, fast-paced twenties were over, and he was now the same age as Papa Clark and Papa Craig when they met and married his mother. The time to settle down, to make a commitment, would approach sooner rather than later. Question was, was he willing to make the commitment with not only one person but two?

For the first time since he was seventeen, Jay allowed his memory to reflect on his father's death and its impact. He remembered the hell Papa Craig and his mother went through, and Jay couldn't imagine being responsible for being the source of hurt in so many people's lives if anything happened to him. Being best friends was one thing, but the bond of being co-husbands was too heavy for Jay to risk losing. He'd decided a few days after his last birthday that he would marry his own wife and have his own children. At least then, he'd only be responsible for one heart instead of two.

Jay had his head bent down, allowing Mr. Davis to edge the back of his head, when Brody's white leather boat shoes appeared in his sight. Did he really have to give him another lecture right now? "Brody, I told you not now. I insist you wait until we're alone."

Brody bent at the knees and squatted in front of Jay to allow their eyes to meet. "Look, Jay, I have to have her. She's our wife, I know it. I knew it the moment she looked at me." Jay was shocked at the desperation in Brody's voice. "I need you to talk to me, brother. If you really love me like I know you do, you'll be honest with me." Brody visibly swallowed before asking, "Do you still want to have a family with me?"

Great fucking timing. The entire barbershop was now staring at them, anticipating. When the hell did So Fresh turn into Luscious? Jay took in a deep breath and replied, "No. No, buddy, I don't. I've decided to build a family of my own. I'm sorry."

His heart ached as he watched Brody's head drop and his eyes shut tight. He was obviously distraught from the news, but he only took a few seconds to compose himself.

"All right, then, I respect your decision," Brody finally said when he looked back at him. He was lying through his teeth. His face looked devoid of emotion, but Jay could read his eyes like an open book. In them swam pain, heartbreak, and disappointment. "I haven't changed my mind about Taylor, though. I'll use everything in my power to have her hand by the end of the summer. But I need your help, Jay."

"She's going to be your bride, Brody. That hardly concerns me."

"Oh, but it does. I didn't miss the way she looked at you, the way her tiny body shivered from the slightest touch of your hand." Brody let out a long breath, shaking his head. "She probably was badly hurt by that jerk and she's pushing away because she's frightened. She will be mine, but I can't tear down her walls alone, Jay. I need you."

Chapter 3

Taylor woke up the next morning to the delicious faint smell of bacon coming from the kitchen. As she slowly opened her eyes, she could see that her window was wide open, letting in a pool of summer sunshine from the bright sky. She sat up and stretched, inhaling the fresh smell of the morning dew, and then she suddenly remembered her encounter with Brody and Jay.

"Ugh, just what I need," she mumbled as she slipped on her fuzzy marabou house slippers. Brody and Jay were the most beautiful men she had ever seen. But that was the problem. Their couture jeans, gelled hair, and over-priced T-shirts weren't going to charm her into being a fool yet again.

Before meeting Dillon, she had avoided those kinds of men like the plague. She grew up watching her friends drop like flies at the sight of any Dallas douche bag with a pretty face and flashy car, only to be thrown away like a sticky used tissue.

The night she met Dillon at the annual HCM charity ball, he spent the night following her around the party, doing his best to charm his way to a date with "the most angelic beauty queen in Dallas." She remembered rolling her eyes at his cheesy, one-size-fits-all lines.

After leaving her office the next day, she found him sitting cross legged on the hood of her car. Before she'd had a chance to protest, he had begun to croon "Will You Still Love Me Tomorrow?" as he strummed his acoustic guitar like a shaggy-haired white knight. She had known Dillon was a playboy, but no man had ever sung for her, and his voice was so sweet, so innocent. She had completely fallen for it. Such a fool!

When Taylor walked into the kitchen, she found a white china plate piled with thick-cut bacon, jalapeño cheese grits, and biscuits with country gravy. It was the same breakfast her father would make her on Sunday mornings, his only day off. Beside the plate was a note from Aunt Veronica.

Good morning, Baby Girl!
Enjoy your breakfast, and then meet me and the girls at Luscious for mani-pedis.
Xoxo,
Auntie Veronica

Taylor looked up at the clock. 9:33 AM. If she didn't get her ass up and out, she'd likely just sit around pathetically daydreaming about the ménage that could never be. Sighing inwardly, Taylor reminded herself it was better safe than sorry.

After finishing her breakfast and morning shower, Taylor stood in her closet, staring at her clothes in frustration. She silently wished for a day when she could actually be *overwhelmed* by her closet. After a few moments, she settled on a sleeveless, white cotton eyelet sundress with thick straps, a scoop neck, and a corseted bodice, and for shoes she decided on her yellow Kate Spade cork wedges. She wanted to be sexy but didn't want to look like she was trying too hard or expecting too much. In fact, she promised herself right then to not expect anything at all. "They're just two local gentlemen looking to show the new girl around town, that's all."

Taylor worked fast on her hair and makeup, so she was out the door and on her way to Luscious Beauty Spa in less than an hour.

Luscious was her aunt's everyday hangout. Any day of the week, before The Boom Boom Room opened at 9 p.m., Aunt Veronica could be found there with her three closest friends, Aurora Compton-Blanc, Greta McCall, and Beverly Cullen.

The beauty shop was owned by Aurora who received the spa as a wedding gift when she married Robert Compton and his best friend, Frederick Blanc, twenty-five years ago. Although she was only twenty at the time, Aurora had insisted on her own business to keep her busy while her husbands operated Stephanie & Co. Stephanie was the two-story jewelry boutique located downtown. It sold high-end jewelry while the adjoining outdoor café, Breakfast at Stephanie's, overlooked the square and was a legendary Sunday brunch favorite with the locals. Taylor thought they served the best vanilla French toast she'd ever tried.

"Mornin', baby girl!" Taylor was greeted by Aunt Veronica's booming voice as she walked into Luscious. The other four women occupying the salon followed with their own enthusiastic good mornings. The salon was set up like an elegant, vintage beauty shop. It had soft pink walls adorned with framed silhouettes of girls with up-dos, and it was encircled with white mod swivel chairs for the clients.

"Why, clutch the pearls! Aren't you a *vision*?" Aurora dramatically brought her hand to her throat as she looked over Taylor. She was adorned with her signature fur-collared robe. Her chin-length, blond hair still had a few hot rollers scattered throughout.

Suddenly, Beverly threw down her copy of the day's *Dallas Times* and scurried across the salon floor to get within a few inches of Taylor's face as though she were examining a squashed bug. "Oh, my Lord! Veronica, she's met a man."

Taylor's cheeks grew hot at Beverly's incredible intuition. Beverly was a pit-bull in a skirt, holding a parasol. As a single mother of four grown sons, Beverly was a straight-shooter with eyes in the back of her head and the instincts of a mama grizzly.

"Aaaaahhhh!" Taylor flinched from the ear-piercing squeal as Aunt Veronica hopped up from her salon chair and ran to embrace Taylor. Taylor couldn't help but laugh at her aunt's endearing excitement. She reached up to embrace the back of Aunt Veronica's head, but she still had scattered foils hanging throughout her dark brown hair.

"So, who's the lucky gentleman, baby?" asked Aunt Veronica when she released Taylor from her death-grip of a hug.

"Brody Bartlett," said Taylor, then she continued despite the wide-eyes staring back at her, "and Jay Stephens." The room filled with dramatic, feminine gasps and whispers.

"Well, I'll be damned, girl." Beverly cocked up an eyebrow as she rested her hands on her full hips, failing to hide the smirk forming on her scarlet lips.

"You know, sugar," began Greta, who was still staring at her reflection in the back of the room as she teased her short red hair, "if you plan to keep up with those two, you better put in some time with a little yoga."

Greta quickly spun in her salon chair to face the women and effortlessly pulled both legs behind her head in a flash. "Trust me, sugar, you'll thank me." Her face beamed with pride.

Aurora began to eagerly clap as Veronica and Beverly just rolled their eyes and groaned. When Aurora didn't stop clapping after a few short seconds, Beverly slapped Aurora's hands and snapped, "Aurora, *please*! It's the same damn trick she shows off to everyone."

"But it never fails to impress me," Aurora remarked sweetly.

Greta was the quintessential cougar. Despite being the oldest of the bunch at fifty-five, she was still built like a Coke bottle and radiated more confidence than any of the twenty-something club rats Taylor knew in Dallas.

Greta owned the yoga studio, Wet Lotus, down the street. She specialized in Bikram yoga which involved heating a room to over a hundred degrees to encourage clients to sweat as they practiced their moves. Greta was also the wife of the wealthy McCall triplets. Naturally, they were fifteen years her junior.

Clearing her throat, Taylor remarked, "Honestly, it's not that big of a deal. I just have a tiny crush on a couple of local boys, is all.

There's nothing more to it, and I'm set on making sure it stays that way."

Aunt Veronica's eyes widened with shock. "Oh, baby girl, just a couple of local boys?" Taylor looked around the salon in confusion when all the women started to giggle. "That's the last thing Brody Bartlett and Jay Stephens are."

"What do you mean?" This was all getting a little too weird for Taylor. Her eyes bounced around the room as the women randomly took turns giving her a piece of the men's history.

"Baby girl, you don't recognize them? Brody Bartlett is the heir to the Bartlett family fortune. The Bartletts were one of Male Order's five founding families."

"Their ancestors moved to Texas after strikin' gold in California in the early 1900s then invested in the railroad industry."

"Jay and Brody have been inseparable since they were knee-high to a grasshopper."

"They sold their own social networking Web site for twelve billion dollars just this past year."

"Twelve *billion* dollars." Taylor gasped.

"They're billionaires, sugar."

"Only, Brody was already a billionaire before the Web site."

Her brain tried to grasp the concept of what they were feeding her. "Billionaires?" She thought their names sounded familiar when she met them, but Taylor was always too caught up in the mix of Dallas drama and charity events to be concerned with West Coast gossip.

"Yes, honey, *billionaires*." Aunt Veronica's stare suddenly swayed from Taylor's eyes to behind her back. "Why, good mornin', gentlemen."

* * * *

"Good morning, ladies," both men chimed in at the same time. The smooth, melodious unity in Jay's and Brody's voices immediately made Taylor's nipples harden against the soft cotton of her sundress before she could even turn around to face them. She waited for the eager greetings from the beauty shop patrons to end and for the belligerent butterflies in her stomach to calm down.

Using a moment to take a nervous breath, she then turned to face the men she hadn't stopped thinking about since they'd interrupted her sunbathing. And goddamn it, they were even more gorgeous and taller than she remembered. She'd spent the last day imagining the breathtaking beauty of their faces and the sexy contours of their bodies over and over again, but her memory gave no justice to the gods of perfection she now looked at.

Jay wore a dark gray, short-sleeved, button-down shirt made of a cotton fabric so light Taylor could see his black under-tank showing through. His army-green cargo shorts hit just below his knees, and he wore leather boat shoes that were the same shade as his shirt.

Brody's shirt looked like it was made of the same thin fabric as Jay's, but Brody's was white with long sleeves that were rolled up just above his elbows, just enough for his incredible biceps to show. He wore long, powder-blue cotton shorts with navy leather flip-flops.

Although she stood several feet away, Taylor could smell the freshness and enticing men's scented bodywash that still clung to their skin from the showers they must had just taken, judging from their damp hair. Their clean scent had Taylor aching to sniff and taste every inch of their powerful bodies.

"Brody and I came to have a word with Miss Ewing," Jay said, directing it more toward Veronica, out of respect, Taylor assumed.

"Well, I declare, my niece sure is a lucky young lady. What did y'all have planned for my gorgeous, smart, talented, caring baby girl?"

"Auntie!" Taylor scolded in embarrassment. She wanted to crawl under a rock. Aunt Veronica continued to stare at the men as though she hadn't heard Taylor.

Jay and Brody laughed at Aunt Veronica's shameless plug. "We want to talk a little business with Miss Ewing," said Brody. "Our families have been looking for a new foundation to sponsor, and from what we heard, Miss Ewing's lecture made quite an impact on our football players. In fact, they've all scheduled doctor appointments for heart checkups."

Taylor smiled proudly. To hear it resonated with just one of the students would have meant success, but knowing the entire team scheduled checkups gave Taylor a thrill of victory. It was moments like these that made pageantry worth every moment of the time and effort.

"Shall we?" the men asked together. They both bowed their heads toward her as they asked before splitting apart and making a walkway for Taylor between them. Taylor watched in fascination as the women in the salon all swooned dramatically. At least she wasn't the only woman that became a smitten kitten around them.

After saying their goodbyes, Taylor slightly lifted her dress, and she made her way down the steps of Luscious, nonchalantly using her southern belle mannerisms to mask the fact she was actually clenching her dress to dry her clammy palms on the cotton. She followed Jay and Brody into the gorgeous, bright summer day.

She did her best to calm her nerves by taking deep, slow breaths in and out of her nose without being too obvious about it. But just standing next to the men again, smelling them as the breeze spread their scent, feeling their sensual body heat when they would casually brush past her as they walked, was more than enough to take her breath away.

Standing at the bottom of the salon entrance steps, Taylor turned to the men, cocked a brow, and put her hands on her hips in her best effort to appear sassy and confident. "So what's for lunch?" She attempted to use her best sexy bedroom voice, but it cracked on "-unch." So much for pageant queen poise.

The men exchanged a quick glance and smiled, then Brody replied, "Nothing nearly as decadent as you probably taste, but we'll give our best effort." His friendly voice and the playful wink that followed candy-coated the innuendo, and Taylor didn't try to hold back the smile he inspired.

She'd never thought she would fall for such blatant charm. When the guys at the Dallas dance clubs would approach her, they were as sincere as a used-car salesman looking to pay off a Mafia debt.

Daaaaamn, baby, you look so good, I could put you on a plate and sop you up with a biscuit.

I'm not drunk. I'm just intoxicated by your beauty.

Taylor could vomit her country breakfast right there at the thought of their degrading, chauvinistic approaches. But as smooth as he was, there was something about Brody that made everything he said sound extra genuine.

Maybe she *could* trust them.

Oh, c'mon, Taylor. These men are billionaires*! They probably have every six-foot-tall Brazilian lingerie supermodel on speed dial. Do you really think you could ever actually mean something special to these two?*

When Taylor stopped in her tracks in the parking lot, the men immediately stopped, as well. Brody took a step toward her, his brow furrowed in confusion. "Are you all right, Taylor? You look like you've just seen a damn ghost, honey."

"I'm sorry, gentleman." Taylor hung her head in embarrassment.

She couldn't go on a date with these men. Taylor couldn't deny it. She was wildly attracted to both of them, and she hated herself for being put under their spell.

Just looking at them, from the refined beauty of their faces down their long forms and to their Italian leather Tod's, Taylor doubted these men ever had to know what loneliness or rejection was, and she couldn't imagine they ever would. Taylor could only imagine the number of women that threw themselves at the men on a daily basis. She couldn't allow herself to become just another insecure, self-destructive groupie who was willing to bow at their feet. But she'd better get rid of them soon, then, because she was about to toss her pride and fall to her knees at any moment. "Forgive me, but I can't go to lunch with you."

Taylor watched Jay give a brief nod to Brody, then he turned to look in her eyes. As he slowly walked over to her, she could feel the pulse in her neck beating frantically against her flesh. He reached down and used both of his large hands to envelop her left one. He felt warm and masculine against her cool skin, and she felt the heat spread over her body and pool in her silk thong. Damn their witchery.

"Can I be frank?" she asked before he had a chance to say anything.

"Please." Jay's eyes were focused only on hers.

Taylor broke the eye contact and looked away as she tried to think of the best way to explain herself without coming off as too pathetic. "When I look at you two," she sighed and shook her head as she struggled to find the words, "when you look at me—"

"Look at me, Taylor," Jay commanded, and she obediently gazed into the captivating emeralds. "How about we just worry about the charity today? Maybe we can talk about all the other stuff later, but for now, we want nothing more than to just sit down and get to know you a little better."

He ever so slowly grazed the mound of flesh that covered her heart, forcing her to suck in a sharp breath of pleasure. She felt the goose bumps form across her skin, sending an electric wave of sensation straight to her peaked nipples. He smiled as if he knew what kind of effect he had on her. "What do you say?"

With a little bit off the pressure lifted off her shoulders, Taylor took a deep breath, nodded, and followed them to their white truck.

* * * *

Taylor marveled at the modern extravagance that breathed through Hester's Steakhouse. They walked in to a curtain of lovely music coming from the piano man playing in the back of the restaurant. As they walked toward the hostess stand to the right of the room, Taylor took a moment to glance around. In front of them was a large layout of intimate round tables with a lit tea light in the center of each one. In the back of the room was the rounded bar, shelves of hundreds of bottles of liquors displayed right behind it. When she looked up, she saw an enormous, ritzy chandelier hung down from the second floor ceiling. The second floor was an open loft that surrounded the hanging chandelier, enabling the customers to view one floor from the other. As she dropped her gaze back down, she noticed the large booths against the side walls. Every booth and table seemed to be the home of a lively conversation.

"Good afternoon, Mr. Stephens," the pretty young hostess nodded her welcome at him then turned to Brody and gave another nod as she continued, "Mr. Bartlett. Would you like your private room?"

"No thank you, Claudine," Brody replied politely. "This is Miss Ewing's first time at Hester's, and we would like her to experience it fully," he indicated the bottom floor with a wave of his hand, "down here."

Claudine smiled. "Yes, sir. Come with me, please."

They were led to a booth in the back with one long bench that rounded the far corner. Taylor slid in first, then the men slid in on either side of her. As Taylor looked around, she saw elegant couples on dates, co-workers on lunch meetings, business men celebrating their latest victories, pretty much anyone who was anyone in Male Order.

The hostess handed them a leather-framed single-page menu before walking off.

"Welcome back, Mr. Bartlett and Mr. Stephens."

Taylor looked up to see a clean-cut young waiter with an impeccable posture and an immaculate uniform. He smiled at Taylor and nodded a greeting before directing his attention back to the men. "The usual, sir?"

Both men nodded slightly, looking completely at ease, their attention focused on her.

Taylor squeezed her thighs together under the table as moisture began to dampen the silky lace patch covering her mound. *Damn it, that happens every time they do that,* Taylor thought in frustration. She cursed her choice of clothing for the day. Her dress wasn't slutty short, but it was short enough to make her worry about the desire that had created a wet spot in her thong.

Jay then turned to his left to face Taylor. "Do you mind?" he politely asked and held his hand out.

"Not at all," she replied and handed him the menu. She couldn't help but feel intrigued by his confidence to order for her.

Jay took Brody's menu, as well, before handing them to the waiter. Taylor didn't doubt this man was definitely used to being the one in charge. "Same entrée for all three. Instead of the sides, we'll have the chef's tasting."

"Yes, sir." The waiter gave a subtle bow of his head before walking away.

"So are you enjoying your little vacation here in Male Order so far?" Brody asked.

"I am, thank you. Although, I admit I haven't done much but sunbathe as I escape in my Charlotte Brontë novels."

"Doesn't sound so bad to me," Brody said with a beautiful smile

"It's actually been quite divine," Taylor confessed.

"So you haven't been going down to The Boom Boom Room during the evenings?" Jay asked as he slightly leaned in, seeming particularly interested in her response.

"I'm afraid that after all the tedious clubbing nights back in Dallas, I have little motivation to go out. Most of the time I'm watching *Mission: Vogue* reruns on cable. If I really feel like getting out, Aunt Veronica and I usually have a girls' day where we walk around SoMale to window shop and eat sushi." She probably sounded like a tired wet towel, but she had to be honest.

Just then, the waiter returned with a large tray that held three plates. Behind him was an army of other wait staff, each holding trays of several small, metal ramekins of various sides. A perfectly cut, juicy prime rib was placed in front of her.

"A medium-rare prime rib with a dollop of horseradish garlic butter on the far left side of your plate," their waiter explained before stepping to the side to allow the other waiters to step forward. The rest took turns pointing out the au gratin potatoes, white cheddar macaroni and cheese, almond asparagus, bourbon sweet potatoes, and several types of steamed vegetables before leaving them to enjoy.

The meal was the most succulent she had ever had. They three of them barely spoke during the first several minutes. While they ate, they talked about the upcoming college football season, which they were all more than excited about.

"I'm so jealous, I can't believe you have premium club seating every year," Taylor gushed in awe.

Brody reached over and squeezed her hand. "I'd love to take you to as many games as you'd like this season." He grinned, then continued, "Or any other season, for that matter."

And like that, Brody again had her heart racing with excitement with just a few words.

"This place has yet to fail me," said Jay as he popped the last bite of his steak in his mouth. The moment he placed his linen napkin on the plate, the waiter was back at their table to take away their empty plates.

"Would you like to order anything from our dessert menu?"

Both men vigorously shook their heads no, their hands waving in defeat. She might come off prim and proper, but Taylor had never been the kind of girl to turn away a dessert.

"I'll have the chocolate volcano, with an extra scoop of ice cream, please. Thank you so much". Taylor handed the menu back to the waiter then noticed the shocked faces of Jay and Brody on either side of her. She couldn't help but laugh. "What? Not every pageant queen is on the all-you-can-eat Xanax and Tic Tac diet."

The men looked at each other and began to laugh at the same time.

They really need to stop doing that. Taylor once again felt a deep ache in her pussy and adjusted in her seat to allow her thighs to squeeze tighter, temporarily relieving the ache radiating from her core. She could now feel her nipples tighten, pushing against the lace material of her top.

"Well, that's definitely a first. A woman that can eat more than us." Taylor playfully slapped Brody's shoulder, glaring at his remark as she fought to keep a smile off her face.

"I don't mean to interrupt your fun, but shall we move on to what exactly you two had in mind for the foundation?"

Both men sat up straighter, and Jay began. "Grayson and Gavin said your father died from HCM when you were twelve. That must have been tough on you and your mom."

"Extremely." She smiled a thanks to the waiter as he placed the giant dessert on the table. "To be honest, I expected them to be tough on me, but the boys were extremely polite and paid close attention to the lecture."

"Well, Taylor," Brody's warm gaze bounced to her cleavage before returning to her face, "to say you are enchanting would be a devastating understatement."

Taylor's eyes retreated to the gooey chocolate pile before her, and she felt her face blush with heat. "You're being nice."

"He's being honest," Jay abruptly shot back. Taylor stared at him, and the admiring look he gave her made her stomach flutter with giddiness. "As I was saying," he continued, shifting his concentration to doctoring up the large coffee placed in front of him, "the twins were quite convincing when they explained why Brody and I should donate to the HCM awareness tour you plan to conduct this year for Dallas-area grade schools." He steadily poured a cascade of sugar into his coffee as he spoke.

"Yes, if we can get the funding, I know the tour can save lives. HCM is the leading cause for sudden cardiac deaths among young athletes. If we can encourage students and their parents to test for heart abnormalities, we can prevent a lot of those cases." She noticed Jay had been staring at her lips their entire time she spoke. "What?"

"Nothing," he replied flatly before taking a large gulp of his beverage. She wondered what he had been thinking. "Our young athletes are an important part of the Male Order community. We want what's best for them. Would five million be sufficient?" He nodded to Brody who then pulled out a checkbook from his pants pocket.

"*F-f-five* million?" Taylor could hardly get the words out of her mouth through her shock.

Jay winked at her as he sipped from the giant mug. "You're right. Make it ten."

Brody casually scribbled through the check he had begun to fill out and started on a new one.

Taylor shook her head in astonishment when Brody handed her the completed check. "This is incredibly generous, Mr. Stephens and Mr. Bartlett. How can I even begin to thank you?"

Brody laughed softly. "Taylor, stop. Just because we're doing business together doesn't mean we don't like hearing our names on those luscious lips. It's still Brody and Jay, please."

"Of course." Taylor's heart skipped. She had underestimated the size of their hearts. She was so giddy about the donation, she didn't hesitate to reach out and grab their hands. "Thank you so much, Jay and Brody. From the bottom of my heart, thank you." She swallowed to fight the tears forming in her eyes, but she felt a slight tickle as two trickled down her cheek.

"Oh, Taylor," Jay whispered as he reached to wipe her tears. His eyes bore into her as his large palm rested on her cheek. Yes, she definitely knew it now. She could feel it in every fiber of her being. He wanted her just as she wanted him. They both did. Her palms sweated, and she could practically hear her heart racing dangerously. She held the eye contact, and her head felt heavy as she leaned into his touch. He visibly swallowed and inhaled deeply.

"There y'all are! We have been looking all over for you two." The whiney, high-pitched voice broke through Taylor's trance. She looked over to see two young women sashaying over to their booth from the bar like two hungry bobcats that had spotted a couple of wounded jackrabbits.

The one that spoke wore a much too tight red dress that looked like it was painted on. Her bleached, overly processed hair had huge chunks of black streaks, and she toyed with her tongue ring as she gave each man a slow onceover. The other woman had a similar hairstyle, only hers was bright red with platinum streaks. She was wearing the same dress as the other woman, only hers was bright white. Taylor winced when she realized the woman chose not to wear a bra under the thin material. They both carried martinis that they frequently took huge gulps of as they talked.

Taylor heard the men curse under their breaths just as the women approached. She released their hands and sat up straighter, attempting to compose herself.

"Good day, Summer," Jay said to the narrow-hipped blonde skunk in red. He nodded politely though his tone sounded like he wasn't too happy to see them.

"Candace." Brody greeted the redheaded fashion victim in white through clenched teeth.

"I go by Candy now, sugar," she corrected.

"Of course you do," Brody mumbled.

"Ladies, this is Miss Taylor Ewing," Jay began. "She's visiting from Dal—"

"Yeah, that's nice," Summer interrupted. "Anyway, Candy and I were curious to see if y'all have decided on your dates for the cotillion this year."

"Still deciding," Jay replied quickly before taking another swig of coffee. "Like we said last year—and the summer before that—if we decide we want to be graced with your presence, you'll be the first to know."

With that, Summer leaned over the table, her lanky forearms pushing Taylor's aside as they rested on the surface. Her face was just inches from the Jay's. Taylor had never been a jealous woman, but she couldn't shake the sudden deep desire to rip out the silver rod of metal in her tongue that continued to blatantly wag at Jay and Brody.

"I'm sure Candy and I can think of a few ways to sway your decision," Summer said as she wiggled her flat backside suggestively.

"Maybe we can even invite our twin cheerleader neighbors over. Technically, seventeen is legal in Texas."

Okay, wow. Taylor had heard more than enough. "Oh! Look at the time. I must be on my way." She moved as quickly as she could to snatch her purse and motioned for Brody to scoot out of the booth.

"Taylor, wait," Brody pleaded.

When he didn't comply to move, Taylor grew angry. "Excuse me, Mr. Bartlett, but I do believe I asked to be excused." She narrowed her eyes at him to show how serious she was about leaving their awful situation. He must have gotten the hint because he broke eye contact in defeat and scooted out the booth to let her out.

"Mr. Bartlett, Mr. Stephens, thank you so much for a lovely lunch." Why was she so upset? Better yet, why was she even surprised?

Jay stood and walked over to her, Skunk Summer nipping at his heels. "Taylor, you barely had a chance to touch your plate," Jay pointed out as he slapped Summer's outstretched hand away just before it made contact with his cheek.

"Again, I deeply appreciate your donation," Taylor continued to ignore their protests, pretending to search for something in her purse to avoid their gazes, "and I'll make certain the Velvet Rope is given the coveted back-cover sponsorship ad in the Miss Dallas Texas Yellow Rose program." She was certain her disappointment was written all over her face, and she needed to escape as soon as possible before they noticed. "Good day, Mr. Stephens and Mr. Bartlett. And I wish you good luck on the cotillion."

* * * *

Brody shifted panicked eyes to Jay. He seemed to struggle to find his words as he continued to shake his head.

The lunch was going exactly as planned until Thing 1 and Thing 2 decided to have a little fun. Summer and Candy came from good families, and they were raised comfortably. A little too comfortably. Although their intentions were to give their daughters the best they could give, in the process, both sets of parents had created spoiled brats who grew up to be manipulating monsters. Both had been cut off from their family fortunes several months ago after they were busted trying to smuggle cocaine using Summer's father's helicopter. They both had to move out of their new penthouse to come stay in their guest houses, right in time for the cotillion, of course.

He hadn't missed the look in Taylor's eyes when she briefly glanced at him to say good day. He couldn't sense any anger from her, only pain and disappointment. She must have thought they were just common douche bags.

"I guess Miss Shit Don't Stink Dallas Texas was a little upset about something," Summer coldly stated. "Maybe she had a doctor's appointment to get that stick out of her ass."

"Oh my God, please stop talking," Brody said angrily, rubbing little circles over his temples with his fingers.

"We were just having a little fun," Candace said as she downed the last of her gin then popped the olive in her mouth. "We had to make sure she was good enough for our exes."

"Your exes?" Brody gave the women a disgusted look. "We took you to a dance in the eighth grade, and the only thing exchanged that night was a couple of sloppy, awkward kisses at your front doors. That was well before you two began giving the boys tag-team blowjobs behind the bleachers in exchange for their mothers' prescription pills."

Summer laughed. "Oh, please. You really think she's better than us just because she wears pearls and donates Daddy's money to a school for retards?"

"Everything that woman has given to her community was the result of hard work and dedication," Brody protested, "not from stealing or lying on her back."

"Ha! Don't fool yourselves, boys," Summer retorted. "Wearing pastels doesn't mean she's any less adventurous than we are. I saw the way she looked at you two. I know all about women like her."

"You know *nothing* about being a woman," Jay snapped through a clenched jaw. Gasps were heard throughout the tables closest to them. Summer's mouth dropped open in shock, then she narrowed her dark-encircled eyes right at him. Brody looked surprised, too, but it was probably because he never expected Jay to stand up to Summer and Candace in front of the entire town. He just nodded and gave Jay a wide, proud grin.

"Ugh, Sandra Dee was even snobbier than I expected," said Candace, not bothering to be discreet as she appeared to examine her nostrils for traces of cocaine with the compact she retrieved from her purse. "I swear, some people can be so tacky."

Jay struggled to keep his voice low when he stepped up to the women. "If you want to talk about tact, maybe the two of you should salvage what little dignity you have and find some other guys to nauseate. I understand it's a little out of your comfort zone, but mind your own business, get a job, find a decent dress, and try to act like ladies. This is Male Order, for crying out loud. Have a little respect."

He felt Brody's hand on his shoulder as they strolled out of the diner, leaving behind a laughing bartender.

Chapter 4

"Double Southern Comfort sour, please," Taylor called out over Heart's "Magic Man" playing on the jukebox. The blonde behind the bar returned shortly and handed Taylor her drink. By the time she walked back to the corner table where Veronica and her Luscious posse sat, she had already sucked down half of her cocktail.

"Ooh wee! Look at that ass," Veronica exclaimed, indicating the raven-haired stud bending over one of the pool tables while he took his turn in the game.

"He's okay," Taylor said quietly, not bothering to get a real good look at him.

"It's Male Order, baby girl." Greta swayed in her seat to the upbeat melody. "No such thing as a man that's just 'okay.'"

"Now there's a cowboy I'd love to saddle up and ride all night," said Beverley as she blatantly gawked at the masculine denim-clad ass laid out before them. "And when I'm done with him, I'll just bite that cute little head off. *Argh*!" Beverley jokingly took a big bite of the air as she growled, and Taylor almost spewed her liquor all over the table as she joined the gang in a loud bout of laughter.

Taylor watched the four dancing women at the table and wondered how she had ever doubted a Friday night at the Boom Boom Room could ever be this fun. Since the humiliating encounter at Hester's the day before, she had refused to leave Veronica's house in fear of running into Jay and Brody. They had called four times since then, but she had nothing to say to them. Instead, she chose to send them a tray of homemade cookies and a fruit basket along with the thank you note she promised.

She was beyond grateful for their donation to her HCM foundation. Her development chairman broke down in tears of joy when she called to break the great news. That money was going to make all the hopes and dreams Taylor had for her foundation come true.

Yet there could never be anything between her and the two beautiful earth ghosts that haunted her thoughts. She had realized that at the diner. The old brats, Summer and Candy, had made sure of that. Although they had been cruel, they were right. Taylor could never be enough for Brody and Jay. These were men who built an empire based on their "so many women, so little time" worldview.

A hot pink shot lit in a blue flame was placed before her. Taylor looked up to see Aurora's kind baby blues. "It's a Heartbreaker, my own little concoction of bubblegum vodka, raspberry liqueur, cranberry juice, a splash of pineapple, and a little 151 for the fire. It's actually pretty disgusting, but it looks precious and gets the job done." She raised her shot glass, and Taylor followed.

"Here's to the men that we love," Aurora began, and Taylor grinned, immediately recognizing the words. All five women at the table continued in unison, "And here's to the men who love us. But the men that we love never love us, so fuck all the men, and here's to us!" They threw back their heads, drained the liquid, then slammed their empty shot glasses on the table before they all let out a loud *woo-hoo*.

"Thank you all so much for dragging me out. I'm really glad I came."

"I just don't get it, baby girl," said Veronica. "You said for yourself Brody and Jay had been nothing but gentlemen to you. Why on earth would you turn that away?"

"Auntie, it's more complicated than that. Jay and Brody, they're living every man's fantasy right now. They have bottomless bank accounts, extraordinary beauty, and the entire female population hunting them down. What men would be willing to give that all up for just one woman?"

"Mine," replied Aurora.

"And mine," said Greta.

"And mine!" They all looked over to the beautiful, full-figured woman surrounded by five smiling men at the next table. A dozen or so lavender Stephanie boxes and a half-eaten birthday cake sat in front of her. The men continued to take turns feeding the cake to busty blonde.

Taylor sighed in defeat.

"You're punishing them for what Dillon did to you," Veronica pointed out.

"I'm protecting myself, Aunt Veronica."

"Oh, child, *please!*" exclaimed Beverley with a roll of her eyes. "What the hell are you protecting yourself from? Carpel tunnel from their unlimited credit cards? Carpet burn on your knees? An achy back after hours in their bed?"

They all laughed, but Taylor saw their points. She was waving the white flag before she even stepped on the battlefield.

* * * *

"You may want to reconsider a Cuban, so exotic, so forbidden, so rich and sweet." Jay teasingly waved the eight hundred dollar cigar in front of Brody's face.

They had stopped by the men's club for a smoke and drink after their victorious polo match against the Caldwell brothers. Despite the win, the blank, lost look on Brody's face remained as he stared off into the bar mirror on the back wall. "It's helped me, and it'll help you, too." Jay moved the cigar closer.

Brody snatched the cigar from Jay's grip, broke it in half, and threw the remains behind the bar. "For the millionth time, you can't lie to me," he said softly before finishing his bourbon then motioned the bartender for another.

Jay didn't know what else to do but turn his barstool back to face the mirrored wall. He sure as hell couldn't deny it. Over the last couple of days, Jay had forced himself to muster the strength to at least appear unscathed from that afternoon in the diner. He always had a talent for masking his true emotions, but Brody had always been able to see right through it.

They had tried numerous times to reach Taylor, even sending her a half-dozen pairs of Jimmy Choos. Each shoebox also had a sealed, handwritten letter of apology in a different language attached to the outside. They'd figured, what woman—a pageant queen, at that—would be able to resist high-heels and poetry? Apparently, Taylor Ewing. She had kept all the letters, but she sent back the shoeboxes completely unopened. As caring and sweet as she was, she was just as stubborn.

"It hurts, doesn't it?" Brody asked. He turned toward Jay and looked him in the eye. "Say it, Jay. Tell me I'm not the only one."

Jay finished his whiskey in one swallow then rubbed his hand over his face as he braced himself for confession. "Yeah, buddy. It hurts. I see her face every time I close my eyes."

Jay allowed his lids to drift shut, and he could see her clear as day. He remembered how she seemed to glow when she talked about her charity work. The passion she had for helping others oozed through her very being. Her brown eyes sparkled, her beautiful smile lit up her face, and how could he ever forget the way her high, round breasts would rise and fall when she bounced excitedly as she talked about the foundation's future plans.

Jay opened his eyes, but Taylor's sparkling brown eyes continued to stare back. He quickly realized he was staring at their reflection. Taylor made her way through the club and headed toward them. His heart leaped with hope and joy when she smiled.

She was wearing a strapless floral-print dress and black cowboy boots. The crowd parted as she moved closer to the bar. From all the dropped jaws and silenced conversations, Jay would bet every man in the bar was imagining her in nothing but those boots. The image of Taylor lying beneath him played itself in his mind, her cowboy boots resting on his shoulders as he plunged his cock deep inside her pussy while she moaned around Brody's cock.

"She came back to us," he heard Brody whisper beside him. They both turned in their bar stools and stood to face her. There weren't many things that made Jay nervous, but right now, his guts felt like they had fallen to his feet. He felt like jumping up, singing, dancing, and pounding every guy in the bar for the way they looked at her. He fought to abstain from doing all four.

"Good afternoon, gentlemen." Her smile was warm and sincere, but Jay noticed her bottom lip was slightly trembling. She was nervous, a good sign. She wouldn't be nervous if she didn't care, just a little.

"Good afternoon, Taylor. Ravishing as always." Brody sounded as cool as a cucumber. Just seconds ago, Brody had been slumped over the bar like any other hopeless fool in love. Now he radiated his usual cool confidence. "You got a trim, I see. It's lovely."

Taylor looked a little shocked at his observation. "Yes, Aurora thought it would be good for me." Jay saw no difference, but charming the girls was always Brody's role while Jay's was always to persuade the girls to, well, do just about whatever he wanted.

"Every man in this bar is practically on their knees in worship, but I have a feeling it has nothing to do with a two-inch trim." Just as he'd expected, he watched her face turn pink, and she modestly lowered her eyes while her grin spread wider. He'd never guess such a knockout could ever be so humble, but it made his chest tighten in admiration.

"You always insist on making me blush, Jay." Finally hearing his name escape her pink, full lips caused a rush of blood to fall straight to his cock. And my, how beautiful those lips would look wrapped around his thick length.

"Seeing that Jay is too busy imagining inappropriate images of you in those boots, I'll be the gentleman and offer you my seat."

Taylor giggled and briefly dropped her gaze to the growing tent in his khakis as she settled in the stool. "So he is." She bit her bottom lip when her eyes came up to his mouth. Satisfaction ran through him, and he returned her smile.

"I came to apologize. It was rude of me to walk out on lunch like that. You two gave a great gift, and I showed my appreciation by acting like a jealous, ungrateful brat." She took both their hands in hers. "I am so sorry. You gave so much, and I just pouted over wanting more." She took a deep breath and shook her head. "It was selfish, and neither of you deserved that."

Jay turned to Brody and saw he had the same confused look he must've been wearing as well. Her composure and maturity astonished him. Did she just admit to "wanting more"? Where in Heaven had this woman come from? After thirty years of traveling to foreign lands, meeting the most powerful people in the world, and experiencing things most people would only dream of, nothing fascinated him like the woman before him. In contrast to the women of their past, she only got more amazing with each layer they pulled back.

"Do you think you can handle taking a little walk through the woods in those boots," Brody indicated to the high-heels. If only real cowgirls actually worked in those.

"I think I can handle *anything* in these boots."

Every man in the room, as well as a couple of waitresses, turned and watched as Taylor swayed her perfect ass out the door.

* * * *

Last night with the girls had proved to be epic. Taylor had walked slash stumbled out of the Boom Boom Room at 2:30 a.m., feeling like a new woman. A drunk woman, but a new one, nonetheless.

They had danced for hours and, much to the horror of the other patrons, sang along to Al Green and Tom Petty until their voices went hoarse. It was the best time she'd had in Male Order thus far.

But somewhere between teaching Aurora the latest D-town boogie and getting her ass handed to her by Greta during a game of darts, the women shared intimate tales of love and loss.

She'd listened intently as Aurora and Greta told stories and gave advice on being involved in a ménage. Beverley kept her advice general, avoiding the details of her marriage with her late husbands. Taylor got the hint not to push for any.

"When you have two of the most gorgeous, wealthiest men you've ever met willing to share your bed, the most important thing to remember is you are your own worst enemy," Greta had advised. "Trust me, baby girl. With men like ours, you'll never have to be reminded how lucky you are to have them. They tend to not let you forget. In my case, they remind me about three times a day.

"But what you do need to keep in mind is how lucky *they* are. Sure, they can spend all day and night telling you how much they love each and every part of your body and soul, which they will, but you have to convince yourself you deserve the best before you believe any man.

"Women nowadays are so used to being independent our first reaction to a man taking care of us, of cherishing us, is either guilt or defiance," Greta had said. "Being the controlling bitch I am, you can imagine it took a lot of adjusting on my part. My independence was a big part of who I was. I think back on my life as a young woman, before the devoted men or the paid bills, and I am so proud of just how much I survived, how far I've come. And that's when I realized, you know what? If anyone in that damn household deserved to be pampered and worshiped, it was me. You've paid your dues, Taylor. Now it's time to reward yourself."

She'd never thought she would ever receive such support for such a bizarre arrangement.

We both know they'll only leave you. Taylor quickly attempted to distract herself from the pessimistic little devil resting on her shoulder.

"Those things look like a pair of stilts." Jay looked concerned, eyeing her Jessica Simpson cowboy boots.

"I'm a Dallas girl. These are practically house shoes compared to what I'm used to."

She followed them down an intricately paved path that wound through the town woods. She realized it was the first time she'd seen Jay and Brody looking less than immaculate. Their clothes and hair had always been in perfect place. But seeing their hair ruffled, their polo uniforms wrinkled and thoroughly worn in, the enticing scent of male and fresh-cut grass softly radiating from their bodies, she ached to feel herself trapped between them more than ever before.

Taylor's panties grew damp as she inhaled their addicting scent. She'd likely drive herself insane with need if she didn't try to distract her moist pussy.

"Is it true you developed the idea for the Velvet Rope when you started losing track of all the women you were seeing?"

"Well," started Jay, catching up to her side, "not exactly. We decided in economics class when we were sixteen that we would create an empire that would earn us our own names. Together."

Taylor noticed Jay's failed attempt to discreetly rake her body with his eyes as he said the last word. He seemed to suddenly be too deep in thought to realize how obvious he was being. Taylor pretended not to notice, and she continued to follow Brody's lead. Jay stayed by her side, occasionally offering a hand when she had to step over a large log or rock.

This must be the chivalry thing I've heard about once or twice. In her experiences, it was rare to meet a courteous young man who made it a habit to open a lady's car door or allow a woman to enter a room before them or even give their date the chance to order first at a restaurant, for Christ's sake.

* * * *

Brody slightly turned his face over his shoulder as he hiked down the path. "Whether we were dominating on the field or in the boardroom, Jay and I have always been a natural team."

Brody still remembered the day they met. They were five years old and were on the same peewee football team. They'd quickly learned to play off each other's strengths to win the game.

Even then, Jay was fearless and committed. He taught Brody to use his passion for the sport to surrender his fear of failure. The Bartlett name was no doubt a blessing, but it also had him craving his own identity and successes.

"And I was a pretty serious kid at times, but Brody would make it his personal mission to get me to crack a grin. There's always been something about him that encouraged me to just live in the moment. He reminds me that in order to live life to the fullest, you must be present, here in the moment, taking each step of the day as though you're savoring the best flavor you've ever tasted."

Although Taylor tried to keep her eyes on the ground, making sure to not trip in her tall boots, she could feel Jay staring at her as he spoke. When she turned to meet his eyes, he quickly looked away. There seemed to be something weighing heavy on Jay's mind, and Taylor couldn't help but feel he was keeping her at an emotional distance. *Yeah, dumbass, he's a yummy billionaire at thirty who could bed any starlet in Hollywood. Why in hell would you expect something different?*

As they walked, Taylor noticed a heavy floral scent growing stronger with each step she took. "What is that heavenly smell? I just want to wrap myself in it." Closing her eyes, she lifted her chin and inhaled the aroma.

"Magnolia trees." Brody turned to her to give her a full smile as he walked backwards for a few feet, then he turned back around and jogged deeper into the grove.

Suddenly, millions of magnolia blossoms scattered throughout the tree branches came into view. Taylor let out a soft gasp. *My heavens, bless my sight.* She couldn't dream of anything more magnificent.

Brody reached up, plucked a large white bloom, and then handed it to her, allowing his fingers to slowly brush against the back of her hand. His soft touch and his sexy smirk caused her insides to flood with belligerent butterflies, making Taylor shudder in excitement. His amber brown eyes bore into hers, and a knot of emotion clogged Taylor's windpipe.

Brody visibly swallowed then breathed. "My, my, Miss Ewing. Your lips are just about the prettiest things I've ever seen, like a plump, cherry-colored heart." Taylor smiled and looked down at her feet as felt the blush return to her cheeks.

She looked up to thank him, but then she saw a glimpse of something tantalizingly colorful through the trees. She took a few steps, trying to peer through the forest of trunks to get a better look. Frustrated, she brushed past Brody then took off in the best run she could manage in her boots. .

She burst through the grove of trees to discover a huge, calm lake with a pier extending far out from the grass, seducing its onlooker with an open invitation to the delicious water. The body of water was surrounded with neon green and dark green, sprinkled with pinks and purples, yellows and blues, the foliage serving as a magical picture frame to the lake's magnificently raw beauty. There was even a rope swing hanging from one of the tree branches hovering over the lake. Downtown Dallas couldn't hold a candle to its organic glow.

She felt the men come to a sudden halt beside her.

"Oh, wow," she said under her breath. Then something completely unexpected and completely out of character happened to Taylor. A rush of giddiness suddenly swept through her as she stared out into the scene.

When her father was alive, they would wake up at four o'clock in the morning every Sunday to go fishing after their country breakfast, followed by a shotgun lesson in an isolated field. It was their very own quality time, just the two of them, no nagging Mama, no ESPN, and no backbreaking job to steal her daddy away.

Then, images of the life she'd lived for the past twelve years began to flash through her mind. Lying out at the W hotel pool, going on exotic vacations only to be isolated in a fancy resort with other Americans. Hell, the only outdoor activity her pageant Dallas clique would agree to was tennis. But, at the country club, of course. Oh, and it had to be the indoor court on hot days so their makeup wouldn't melt off. Since her father's death, she had yet to enjoy the pure, candid, untainted beauty of nature, and she felt overwhelmingly devastated at the thought.

Then Brody's husky voice echoed in her mind. *In order to live life to the fullest, you must be present, here in the moment.* His words were like a new pair of glasses. Taylor realized that, despite her efforts to shield her heart since her daddy's death, she wasn't any happier today than she was then. Her system of prioritizing awards, trophies, and the wellbeing of others over her own emotional health definitely didn't feel like it was very healthy.

But Brody gave her the answer to her problems with that one line. Instead of thinking about home, her mother's approval, Amber's exhausting drama, her reputation, or contemplating the risk of loving someone, she would surrender herself to the *now*. Whatever the outcome would be with Jay and Brody, whatever their intentions may be, Taylor decided she would give herself permission to enjoy right here, right now.

She couldn't help but laugh aloud, causing confused looks on the men that stood beside her. She didn't even announce what she was laughing at, but they smiled in response anyway.

Taylor then quickly reached down and removed her new boots then she placed Brody's velvety magnolia safely inside one. Taking one more good look at the exquisite image before her, then at those standing beside her, she lifted her dress over her head, tossed it aside, and ran toward the lake.

* * * *

"Let's jump in!" As Taylor made her way down the pier, she occasionally looked over her right shoulder to show them her giggling face as ran to the water wearing only her matching white lace thong and strapless bra.

"Fuck," whispered Brody, his blood immediately flowing to his dick as he took in the image of Taylor's tan, flawless little bubble butt bouncing in bright white lace as she ran to the water. He never saw an ass as perfectly plumped, yet toned, as Taylor's. "I have died and gone to fucking Heaven. Well," Brody paused as he turned to Jay, "hopefully, we will be fucking Heaven soon."

Jay started to laugh and shake his head, but Brody was off, running to the water instead of waiting for a response. Brody continued to watch as Taylor briefly paused at the edge to take a final look back then glided through the air in a graceful dive.

Brody gave absolutely no hesitation. Just as he saw his Taylor swim back up to the surface, he stripped down to his boxers then jumped in. "*Woo hoo!*" His cannonball resulted in a huge splash, and a loud shriek of joy from Taylor. He resurfaced a few inches in front of her face, causing Taylor to break into hysterical laughter as he shook out the water from his hair and onto her. He smiled widely as he watched a drop of water make its way down her cheek and pause at the tiny brown beauty mark to the right of her upper lip. Taylor was such a classic beauty, just like the bombshells in the old movies his mother watched, simply stunning.

Her smile and her laugh were instant drugs. Her happiness gave him a buzz like nothing he'd ever defiantly experimented with in his past. Brody knew then there would be nothing in the world that could stop him from making sure he had his Taylor fix every day, *for the rest of his life.*

As Taylor's laugh slowly began to settle to a soft giggle, her eyes stared at Brody's mouth, following his tongue as it glided along his lips. He watched as her eyes glazed over with lust and heat, and for the first time, he noticed how the sun reflected swirls of gold in her irises.

Brody reached to touch her face, resting his fingertips on the side of her neck. Taylor closed her eyes and exhaled a soft whimper the moment his skin came into contact with hers. His cock jumped in delight at how surprisingly responsive she was to him.

Brody leaned in, briefly hovering over her flushed, parted lips as he inhaled the scent of the melon-cucumber lotion that still clung to her skin. It would be his first kiss as a man in love, and he wanted to remember every curve of her mouth and the flavor of her tongue.

Using both lips to lightly embrace her bottom lip, Brody started with a small double-suck, and he could already hear a soft moan start to form in the back of her throat. He opened his mouth, inviting Taylor's warm, wet tongue to wedge itself between his lips. He growled deeply as she explored his mouth using random flicking motions mixed with slow, long caresses, sweeter than candy.

He felt his hard-on rub against her stomach as she wrapped her soft, delicate arms around his neck and pressed her billowy chest to his. Her nipples had formed into hard pebbles, and a jolt of heat spread to his balls when she unconsciously brushed across one of his nipples with hers. Brody fisted Taylor's hair as he pulled her deeper into his kiss. She moaned louder as the passion of his caress intensified. Reaching below the water's surface, Brody grabbed

Taylor's ass and lifted her until her lush thighs gripped the sides of his waist. Her skin was even silkier than it looked.

Brody let out a low groan as Taylor took his silent direction and wrapped her smooth, golden legs around his waist. She softly gyrated her hips, torturing him with the tease of the friction. When she dropped her head back, he took it as an invitation to finally, *finally*, taste the perfect, large globes that were peeking above the lace trim of her bra.

He effortlessly lifted her small frame until his view was obscured by the pink nipples poking for release through the bra's white lace. Using his tongue, Brody slowly traced a silky path from the top of her right tit down to her cleavage. He tongue fucked the warm valley for several moments before continuing the path up her left breast. Instead of ending at the top, his tongue made a detour to the edge of lace and pushed it back to taste the nipple that stood at attention underneath. Taylor let out a soft cry as he circled his tongue around the stiff peak.

Needing to taste her again, Brody brought her mouth back down to his, and she immediately dove in for the kiss. Suddenly, Taylor pulled her face away to look up at the pier. Brody only used the opportunity to kiss and lick her neck more. He didn't really care what got her attention. He couldn't stop tasting her.

* * * *

Jay toed off his shoes, peeled off his white T-shirt, and pulled off his shorts before he began to make his walk to the pier in his black boxer briefs. Dead man walking.

He could hear Taylor's laughter, and it gave him a sick feeling in his stomach. Although he'd told himself he just wanted Taylor as a quick fling, getting to know her and seeing her surrender herself to the magic of Male Order right before their eyes, he wondered if he would really be able to stop himself from falling in love with Miss Taylor Ewing.

When he began to walk on the pier, he could see that Brody was kissing her deeply. They kissed like they were running out of time, urgently and desperately. He then watched as Brody lifted Taylor to work his mouth on her full tits, her *amazing* tits. His hard-on almost grew painful as he watched Brody use his tongue to pull Taylor's nipple out of her bra and into his sucking mouth.

Damn, Taylor looked so gorgeous with her head flung back, moaning in ecstasy, her eyes closed as her silky auburn hair cascaded down her back. Too damn gorgeous. For the first time in his life, Jay doubted his abilities to successfully complete a challenge. And he never considered "not falling in love" as much of a challenge. But then there was her.

Jay's toes touched the edge of the pier just as Brody and Taylor began to kiss again. He couldn't help but give his cock a quick, firm squeeze to ease some of the ache that had developed as he watched the nearly naked goddess's sexual hunger deepen with each touch Brody gave her.

Jay reached up to put his fingers on his temples as he squeezed his eyes shut. *Think, Jay, think. Shit! This is fucking emotional suicide.*

"Jay."

Jay's head immediately snapped up at the soft, sensual southern purr of her voice.

"Jay, join us. Please."

Taylor looked up at him with those Goddamn innocent-looking doe eyes. She was almost begging him with that hypnotic stare. The thought of Taylor begging for him on her knees, naked and bound, was almost enough to make him explode all over them right then and there.

Brody continued to shower Taylor's neck with attention since she had released his kiss to talk to Jay. He could see that Brody's intense passion for Taylor was completely unlike any chemistry he had ever witnessed between his friend and a woman.

Brody must have sensed Jay's hesitation. Although he spoke as he rubbed the side of his face against Taylor's naked, beaded nipples, Brody took a break from the kissing to turn his head to Jay. "You're completely in control, Jay. It's whatever you want."

Brody always knew exactly what to say to calm him down.

"So, do you want to get wet with us, Jay?"

But Taylor knew even better.

Looking in her eyes, his gut wrenched as if he were at the top of a rollercoaster loop anticipating the frightening drop below. He took a deep breath and dove in.

* * * *

Taylor couldn't think of a more beautiful image than the look in Jay's eyes when she had asked him to join her. Although she could sense Jay had been holding up an emotional wall since they met, the look in his eyes at that moment was the most vulnerable Jay had been since she'd met him.

Jay's large body landed in the water with a huge splash. She smiled in encouragement as he began to swim his way toward her. Before Taylor realized Brody had swum away, she heard a loud "*Woo hoo!*" and turned to see Brody swinging from the rope swing a few trees down from them. He crashed to the water below.

Taylor suddenly felt the masculine warmth of Jay's body as he moved closer to her, and she whipped around in the water to face him. She prayed her brain was branded with the memory of how beautiful Jay Stephens looked at that moment. Crystal water drops sprinkled his tanned, broad shoulders, his full bottom lip slightly quivering from the chill of the lake, his raven-colored hair dripping a little water down the sides of his face. His jade eyes darkened to an emerald color, but they were no less hypnotizing, especially with the sunrays that shone down and made them sparkle. "Brody never gets this shaken up for just a slice of cherry pie."

"Excuse me?" Taylor's voice seethed with attitude at his disrespectful innuendo. "I'm not a slice cherry of pie, Mr. Stephens."

But instead of apologizing, Jay moved even closer until their faces were just a few inches apart and whispered, "Of course you're not." Jay enveloped her body in his muscular arms, pulling their torsos together as he took her mouth in his. Her already swollen clit throbbed in reaction to the firm, hungry sucking he was giving her tongue. He broke away and looked down at her. "Mmm, but you sure taste like a cherry pie."

Taylor wanted to protest, sass him for being such a pompous barbarian. How dare he compare her to a piece of food. She would never accept such behavior from a man. But the way he drawled *cherry pie* sure was sexy, and the ache deep inside her pussy betrayed her logical thought of slapping him across his face for such talk.

Jay moved closer, his eyes grazing over every exposed inch of her upper body. *Now! Slap the arrogant ape now!* Her brain struggled to scream reason into her consciousness, but oh, he smelled so damn good. He bent his head down, and his tongue began making a slick, winding trail from her jaw line, down the scoop of her neck, and then wedged in the cleavage of her swollen breasts.

She searched for the strength to tell him no, to push him away and take back the control he'd taken from her. All she could manage was a deep moan as he firmly held her by the waist and lifted her body to his face. She gripped his large shoulders, and his mouth slowly tasted her stiff, aroused nipples.

Tell him to stop.

"Don't stop! Oh, Jay, don't stop!" She probably should have been listening to her head, but her bratty pussy was just so much louder.

"If your juice tastes anything like your tongue or tits, I'll never go hungry again."

He lowered her back down, and she immediately felt his enormous erection. He managed to sustain his cool countenance, despite his giant cock jumping against her body as if it were coaxing her body to move in closer.

She then felt Brody's warm hands holding her shoulders from behind. He then gently brushed her hair to the side as he kissed the back of her neck with tiny pecks and warm touches of the tip of his tongue. His warm breath against her wet skin gave her a chill, leaving behind patches of gooseflesh. Never before had Taylor ever lost control of her desire, but being sandwiched between the two gorgeous, sexy best friends wrung the life out any chance she would be able to stop.

She reached back with her left arm while she kept her other wrapped around Jay's neck, then she clenched Brody's hair. The wet, soft waves slipped between her fingers like silk. She moaned in pleasure as the realization of being with two men at once crashed down on Taylor's stunned consciousness.

Jay looked into her eyes as he gathered her breasts from her bra. She felt Brody's giant hands around her waist as he slightly lifted her in the water, giving Jay better access to her tits while Brody softly traced his nose and lips along the curves of her back. Jay let out a deep growl as he pushed her breasts together to capture her nipples in his warm mouth at the same time.

Taylor let her head fall back as she struggled to keep her breath. As Jay sucked her nipples, Brody traced his finger along the strip of lace wedged between her ass cheeks. He started at the top and slowly traced his fingertip down until it reached her hot mound. The aching convulsions occurring in her creaming channel became painful with need. She started to grind her pussy against Jay's rock-hard abs, trying her best to relinquish the torture that drenched her folds.

She couldn't resist reaching down in the water to wrap her hand around the impressive hard-on that fought to rip through Jay's boxer briefs. He hissed air through his teeth at her touch, making Taylor's nipples tingle at the sound of his obvious pleasure.

Jay gripped Taylor's waist, softly digging his fingertips in her back while she slowly stroked up and down his rock-hard length. Her grip glided over his soft skin in the water, and the engorged head of his cock throbbed in her hand. She couldn't remember wanting to taste a man so damn badly, and she licked her lips at the mere thought of his long dick filling her throat.

Taylor gripped her thighs tight around Jay's waist, and she began maneuvering Jay's erection so it rubbed and tapped her clit. She moaned loudly, feeling the large, mushroomed head throb against the sensitive hood. Brody continued to lick the back of her ear, flicking her earlobe with his tongue as he made the hottest husky moans.

The low groans of both men had Taylor wiggling with need. Jay's erection laid flat against her swollen nub, and Brody's hard-on was lying against the lace between her ass cheeks. Their cocks were both incredibly long and wide. Who was bigger seemed to only depend on their individual states of arousal.

She rocked her hips back and forth, allowing both cocks to grind against different parts of her barely covered pussy. The head of Jay's dick teased her pearl through the lace of her panties. Her pussy lips were swollen with desire and were spilling out the sides of her thong, giving Brody access to caress them with his cock from behind.

As Brody kissed the back of her neck, he would thrust against the material between her ass cheeks and up until he would almost touch Jay. They were both beginning to slow down a little, and Taylor sensed they were now struggling to keep control of their excitement.

Both men had one hand on each of her hips. They slowly inched their fingers to the hot area between her shuddering thighs. The combined heat of their skin covered her, and Taylor released a long sigh from the satisfaction of finally having them both touch her pussy as the same time. Each man used two fingers to trace small circles on either side of her clit, and Taylor panted heavily as she rode against their touches.

"Come for us, Taylor," Jay demanded in a husky tone. "We want to see how beautiful you can sound when we really push you over."

"Wait," she panted. "Softer. Please. It's... Oh! It's too much."

Then she felt the sharp clasp of Jay's lips and teeth around a nipple, and just as she was about to scream their names, they were interrupted by the loud splashing of a bunch of college-aged kids down on the other side of the lake.

Taylor pushed herself away from the men, ignoring their frustrated, disappointed curses as she quickly swam under the pier to hide from view. The students didn't seem to have noticed them, so Taylor took the opportunity to swim to the grass and run into the magnolia grove to get dressed. Brody and Jay were not far behind her.

"Like we really need yet another reason to be annoyed by obnoxious frat guys," Brody complained as he pulled his shirt over his head.

Taylor focused on ignoring the painful ache lingering in her pussy, an unpleasant result from not reaching satisfaction after such a long period of buildup. She walked with the men back down the worn path until they were far from the rambunctious pile of testosterone.

"We'll grab you something to eat on the way to your aunt's," Brody said once they reached the road.

"Oh, you don't have to do that, really."

"We insist." Jay's voice was low, but the domination was loud and clear. He must have realized how harsh he sounded because he quickly looked down at Taylor and gave her one of those rare half-smiles then possessively wrapped an arm around her waist as they walked to the truck. Taylor smiled back and walked a little closer to him.

On the way back into town, Brody had called for a pickup order of the chocolate dessert she had ordered a few days ago at Hester's, explaining she needed another chance to finish it since they had been rudely interrupted. The order was waiting for them when they pulled up into Hester's parking lot, the familiar young waiter waiting outside the entrance with a smile on his face.

In just a few short moments, they arrived at Aunt Veronica's walkway. Taylor turned to Brody and Jay, feeling a little awkward while images of their three bodies tangled together in the lake kept popping into her head. "Well, I better go in and shower."

"What's that?" Brody was pointing at something in Veronica's back yard.

Taylor turned her head to see what he was indicating. "Oh, that's the tool shed."

Suddenly, two large bodies were herding her over to the small, windowless shed, each holding an arm in their grips as her small feet shuffled to catch up with their large steps. "Wh-what are you doing?"

"Oh, come on, Taylor," Jay pushed her into the dark storage space, "you didn't really think we would leave you hanging like that, did you? You think I didn't notice you shifting while we were walking over here, trying to get rid of that pain throbbing in your little pink clit?"

"This is crazy. If you want me to invite you in, just say so."

"Where's the fun in that?" Jay suddenly picked her up by the waist and laid her flat on her back on the nearest working table. The doors made a soft thud sound as they sealed shut. The shed was completely dark, and Taylor had no idea which man was where.

"Jay? Brody?" There was just complete silence. She couldn't stop the fear of the unknown from washing panic over her sinking heart.

Taylor tried to get off the table, but two large hands held her firmly down, causing a loud gasp of surprise to escape her lips. The strong hands suddenly started to massage her tits vigorously. She then heard a loud ripping sound as the hands pulled down the neckline of her dress, tearing it half-way down the middle of her torso to gain direct access to her stiff nipples. Someone pinched the exposed buds in excitement, softly then roughly, even softer then even rougher.

"Ooh! Mmm, ow, ooh!" The mystery man groaned at the pleasure and pain he inflicted on her. He pinched down very hard, but the pain only intensified the jolt of electricity sparking its way down to her womb.

Another pair of hands tore away the last scraps of her dress that remained and tore her panties completely off. The action produced another loud ripping of cloth to fill the small, dark shed. The sound unleashed the wanton woman buried inside the southern belle all over again.

"Oh yes! Smell how much I need you." Taylor's hips bucked over and over, desperately searching for a part of their bodies to wet with her cream.

Then she felt one of the men lift both of her hips off the table, gripping her ass as he held her lower half high in the stuffy air. She felt the tip of someone's nose rub against her engorged clit, and then she heard an anonymous, drawn out "mmm" and he sniffed her.

"I want your mouths all over me," Taylor whispered to the figures in the darkness.

She heard two low chuckles from the darkness. They didn't use their voices to answer her. Instead, their teeth began to lightly nip the skin of her ass cheeks and the sides of her breasts.

"Oh, yes, take me any way you want me," she pleaded desperately. She had no idea which man was at what end, but she was already eager to surrender her will to them both. They remained completely silent in response.

Suddenly, she felt a wet, hot mouth against her dripping, convulsing cunt. Taylor's body jerked violently in response to the magical, heavenly tongue that swept its way from between her ass cheeks, up to tongue-fuck her opening, and then she finally screamed out as the firm head strummed against her pulsating pearl.

The heavy man leaning over her chest began jiggling Taylor's tits in his hands as he let her stiff nipples dance over the surface of his face. He moaned primitively as she arched her body closer to him, silently begging him to take her tits for his pleasure. Once she felt his teeth gently clasp down on one nipple while his fingers pinched the other, she immediately felt the sparkling sensation of an orgasm coming on.

Taylor's shrieks grew louder. "Oh, yeah! Yeah, suck me, *both* of you."

The mouth feasting on her folds blew cool air on her heated mound between the vibrating growls he made against her pussy. He sounded like a wild wolf that was having his first meal in days. He slurped and moaned and licked like she was the best thing he ever tasted.

Taylor screamed their names as one hand reached to grip the head between her quaking thighs and the other reached over to the head of curls moving over her swollen nipples.

They both sucked hard as her womb tightened and her peak resuscitated her once-aching heart. Just when she thought her climax would start to recede, the hungry man between her thighs inserted two large fingers in her channel and a moaning mouth bit down on a sore nipple, causing her climax to last several waves longer than she ever thought possible. She ground her pussy against the mouth between her legs until her orgasm passed several moments later.

Taylor continued to lay limp on the table as she struggled to recover from the most intense orgasm she had ever had.

"You sounded so beautiful, baby." She loved how Brody called her 'baby' like it was the most natural thing in the world. They shared a soft kiss in the dark, and then he released her.

"My-My legs feel like jelly," she managed to say between pants of breath.

"Hold on. Don't move." Jay's husky whisper gave her pussy a final shiver. She felt him move up her body, and his tongue wedged between her lips. She softly sucked it until he backed up, as well. She grew more confused when she tasted her desire on *both* their tongues.

Had they tag-teamed devouring her cunt and tits without her even noticing?

Light flooded in the shed for just a brief moment as the men opened the shed door. Jay peeled the large shirt from his body and handed it to her with a soft smile. She pulled it over her torn dress, loving the way she seemed to swim in the giant shirt.

Brody poked his head out the door, scanning left and right. "Okay, looks like the coast is clear."

Before Taylor realized what was happening, Jay lifted her in his arms without a hint of strain. Taylor knew she was a petite girl, but she couldn't help but to be insecure about how heavy she must have been to him. She decided not to protest when Jay began gliding through Aunt Veronica's yard as if he was carrying a feather-light doll.

When they came to the front porch, Jay gently placed her on her feet. Brody was immediately in front of her when her legs gave out. He caught her right before she was going to fall to her knees.

"Whoa there, sugar." Brody kept his hands on either side of her waist as she struggled to maintain balance. She looked up at him, and he was staring at her with tender, loving eyes. She smiled at him and didn't hold back the urge to kiss him. She weaved her fingers through his damp hair as he came in deeper.

Suddenly she was jerked back hard then whipped around to face Jay. He immediately crushed his lips into hers, sending a delicious yearning straight to her clit which caused it to swell right back up. Just as she wrapped her arms around his thick body, he broke their kiss. "Goodnight, Taylor." He then moved to the side, and Brody stepped up to her.

"Goodnight, baby." Brody gave her another brief yet passionate kiss.

She couldn't speak and was barely able to manage to wave goodbye to the men as they walked back to their truck.

Chapter 5

Leaving her damp shoes on the porch, Taylor slowly opened her aunt's front door, poked her head inside, and scanned the area for any trace of Aunt Veronica. Confident she was alone, she quickly tiptoed to the bathroom, doing her best to avoid dripping water on the carpet. Her dress and hair were still pretty wet. Well, not *just* her dress and hair…

Although she was anxious to get some food in her stomach, she was in desperate need of a shower before she could even think of returning to a functioning human being. She started the warm shower and made sure all her bath products were accessible.

She pulled Jay's T-shirt off and looked in the mirror. She giggled at the sight of scattered blades of grass clinging to the curves of her body.

She went over to the hamper to place the shirt inside, but then she hesitated. She looked down at the bundle and pressed the fabric against her nose. Even beneath the heavy smells of sun, grass, and lake water, she could still detect the clean, musky scents of Jay and Brody. She reached down and placed a finger between her pussy lips. Just as she expected, she was dripping wet again for them already. Trying to focus on the mission at hand, she tossed the dress in the hamper and stepped into the tub, doing her best to shake away her lustful thoughts.

The warm shower immediately relaxed her, flowing down her skin, as comforting as a mother's touch. She scrubbed her body with Dove soap as she washed away the day's harsh elements. When she glided the slippery bar of soap over her breasts, her nipples immediately became erect with need, and the memory of Jay's and Brody's hot tongues lapping the tight buds had her pinching her throbbing clit before she even realized her hand had made its way between her legs.

"Oh, stop! You don't need to come every damn few minutes," Taylor scolded herself aloud. Before her pussy could win another argument with her logic, she turned off the hot water and forced herself to stand under the cold shower. Once her horny desire began to subside, she stepped out and dried off.

She applied her melon-cucumber lotion, combed her hair, then walked to her aunt's bedroom wrapped in her towel. She knew Veronica had a large collection of over-sized men shirts under her bed. Taylor scanned through a few before settling on a feather-soft, gray tee with a vintage Cowboys logo on the front. She loved the feeling of the fabric as it brushed against her freshly-shaven thighs.

Taylor walked to the next room where she was staying. She grabbed her laptop off her nightstand and sat on her bed, placing it on her lap as she settled into her usual surfing position.

She hadn't checked her email all week, so there were about twenty unread messages. She scanned through the senders, and she paused on an unfamiliar address. The sender was fairygodmother@stampfree.com, and the message subject was simply "Amber Fox." When she opened it, the only thing in the body of the message was a long link for her to click on. She recognized the Web site's name in the beginning of the link.

Taylor hesitated, not quite sure if she should click on the infamous domain. "Oh, hell, every southern girl has her right to a little gossip on occasion." She clicked on the blue, underlined type before the guilt returned.

The Web site was called Allegedly.com, and it was the Frankenstein of Dallas blogger and socialite, Emilio Estefan. Emilio was a twenty-one-year-old, self-made Dallas celebrity. As the son of immigrant parents from Mexico City, Emilio was raised with the

A Bride for Two Billionaires 77

value of hard work. The result was a Web site that now generated thousands of dollars per ad sale. Last Taylor had heard, that resulted in Emilio receiving about $750,000 per month. Not too bad for a first-generation American citizen.

A youthful, bubbly voice sounded from the laptop speakers. "Hola y howdy. My name is Emilio Estefan. Welcome to Allegedly, your go-to spot for all things trashy, nasty, Dallas, and fabulous. Aye ya yi!"

The Web link had led her to a thread that listed any articles mentioning Amber Fox. Taylor began with an article dating back two days ago.

"Has Amber Fox Had Too Many Cocks?!? Only Emilio has the uncensored pics!"

As Taylor scrolled down, her hand covered her mouth as she gasped in utter horror.

There on the World Wide Web was a collection of paparazzi pictures featuring an obviously inebriated Amber Fox getting out of her BMW, wearing a short pink dress and *no panties*. The paparazzi definitely got their money shot that night. But the most shocking of all was the next picture. It was a close-up of Amber's vagina, covered in oozing open sores!

Taylor shook her head in shock as she brought herself to read the article underneath the pictures.

"Cochina *of the Week" goes to Amber Fox. Looks like Miss Fux-a-lot has been served too much spotted dick pudding. The Miss Dallas Texas Yellow Rose contestant was photographed late Saturday night outside of Plush Lounge as she was getting out of her* ~~tacky~~ *custom pink Beamer. Photogs say Amber parked her car on the curb, spent ten minutes "drinking cola" then crawled out of her car in a drunken stupor.*

Lucky for us, the "Head-Mistress" (as the Cowboys and Mavericks are rumored to affectionately refer to her) has the grace of a redneck truck driver. Little Miss Sophistication gave us a full-on view of her pus-oozing va-jay-jay. (Excuse me, mijitos, *I need to barf...Ok, I'm back.) The word on the street is Amber caught herpes from Daybed* ~~druggie~~ *drummer, Bobby Smalls, who she's been* ~~fucking~~ *dating since beauty-queen/heart disease ambassador Taylor Ewing introduced them backstage at a Daybed concert a couple of months ago...Allegedly!*

Looks like Amber can put those man-made, dick-sucking lips to good use as she kisses her ~~delusional dreams~~ *chances at the crown* adios*!* Cochina!

A few other Amber Fox articles had been posted since, but Taylor had seen enough. She closed her laptop and lay on her back, staring at the ceiling. It was hard for Taylor to feel much sympathy for her old friend, but she never wanted Amber to lose her chances at the title she had been chasing her whole life. Being Miss Dallas Texas Yellow Rose was all Amber cared about, and she was willing to sacrifice everything for it. That included her friendship with Taylor.

For the last year, they had both prepared for the ultimate Texas pageant. But while Taylor spent most of her time volunteering in the name of her hypertrophic cardiomyopathy awareness platform, Amber spent her days drinking at the W pool, and her nights were spent sugar-daddy hunting at every Dallas hotspot.

Over the years, Amber's out-of-control partying had gotten progressively sloppier. What started out as drink-'til-you-blackout binging at fourteen soon turned to suck-it-to-snort-it cocaine clubs at seventeen, then later guess-what-I-am pill highs at twenty-two—and every day since.

But Amber was always this way.

Taylor remembered back when she had first won the Miss Teen Dallas Texas Yellow Rose title. Out of the hundreds of pageant titles a Texas girl could compete for, Miss Teen Dallas Texas Yellow Rose and Miss Dallas Texas Yellow Rose were the most prestigious. Taylor's mother saw the pageant as a great social opportunity for

Taylor, and a great bragging right for herself, mother of a Texas beauty queen.

At first, Taylor refused to consider participating, preferring to devote her free time to the HCM foundation she volunteered for since her father's death. When Daddy had died, the foundation had contacted the family and offered to pay for the funeral her mother couldn't afford. Taylor had always remained incredibly grateful for the help they gave her family during that dark, difficult time. She had also wanted to do her part to prevent others from going through the pain she and her family had to endure.

When Taylor became aware that the pageant allowed each contestant to have a charity platform, and the teen winner's charity would receive two-hundred and fifty thousand dollars, she quickly agreed. For the Miss Dallas Texas Yellow Rose title, the charity donation prize increased to seven-hundred and fifty thousand dollars. That amount now paled in comparison to Jay and Brody's ten-milion dollar donation. Her HCM foundation had recently planned its eleventh statewide tour to educate student athletes on the facts about the disease. She knew with that money, the charity would now be able to take the tour nationwide..

Harold and Amber's father had introduced the girls to each other at the Miss Teen Dallas Texas Yellow Rose participant orientation several months before the pageant. Mr. Fox was a highly respected real estate mogul who specialized in luxury real estate in the Dallas/Fort Worth area. He also had an obsessive hobby of competing in dog shows with his two prized toy poodles, Sir Rush Limbark and Sir Bill O'Bite Me. He was a man of appearance and status, and those priorities were passed down to his pageant-obsessed daughter.

Amber became Taylor's first close friend since she and her mom had entered the Dallas high society. As a pageant girl since the age of nine months, with over a hundred and fifty titles under her belt, Amber had been confident she was a shoo-in for Miss Teen Dallas Texas Yellow Rose, and she made sure every contestant knew it. It wasn't uncommon for one of Amber's rivals to suddenly have a broken high heel or an extra slit down their evening gown.

Taylor had been painfully intimidated with Amber's stunning beauty, especially at such a young, impressionable age. Her skin always had a deep tan, her teeth were snow white, and her voluminous blond hair bounced as she walked. Amber was born a brunette, but her mother began to bleach her hair just a few months before orientation. Amber had explained that, in the pageant world, blondes were more likely to get noticed. But more than anything else, Taylor was enamored by Amber's eyes, a sparkling crystal blue that was kryptonite to any kid's Snack Pack, any teacher's star stickers, and any adult's wallet.

But seven months later, Taylor was crowned the youngest Miss Teen Dallas Texas Yellow Rose at just thirteen, and Amber was runner-up. It was Taylor's first pageant.

Amber went on to win Miss Teen Dallas Texas Cowgirl Spur the next month, but Amber never seemed to get over losing the Miss Teen Dallas Texas Yellow Rose title to a rookie.

Taylor had spent most of her year attending charity events for HCM research. During one event, Taylor and Amber were approached by a boy a few years younger than them.

"I'm very happy to meet you, Miss Teen Dallas Texas Yellow Rose and Miss Teen Dallas Texas Cowgirl Spur." Taylor remembered the young boy's smile beamed with admiration. "I was diagnosed with HCM when I was five, and I just wanted to say thank you for helping people like me. Could y'all please sign my event booklet?"

Taylor remembered the angry fire that danced in Amber's eyes when the boy handed his marker and program to Taylor first. Taylor had pretended not to notice for the boy's sake. "Of course! And the pleasure is all mine! I'm sorry, what did you say your name—" Out of nowhere, Amber grabbed the program out of Taylor's hands and violently tore it to shreds in front of the boy's face. "Hey! Amber, what are you *doing*?"

"Fuck this charity bullshit, and fuck you, dying freak!" Amber screamed at the boy, ignoring Taylor's protests. The young boy ran off in tears.

Amber had called Taylor the next week to apologize for her behavior. "I'm on the rag. You know how it is!" Taylor had felt the social pressure to forgive her friend. After all, she had been there for Taylor when no one else was.

* * * *

Taylor woke up just as her aunt was coming though the bedroom door, holding a tray of sweet tea and a slice of delectable, homemade blueberry pie from the Male Order Diner.

Taylor stretched her arms and let out a satisfied groan.

"Ugh, how long have I been asleep?"

"Just a few hours."

"A few hours? Aunt Veronica, you should've woken me!"

Walking around to Taylor's side of the bed, Aunt Veronica nudged Taylor to learn forward as she rested an extra pillow behind her. "Oh hush now, girl. I done told your simple ass before you got here that if you want to stay with me, I'll make sure you do nothing but rest and relax. No sense in complaining about such a good thing."

Aunt Veronica moved to the other side of the bed and lay on her stomach, her head resting in her hands as she watched Taylor enjoy her evening snack. Finally, Taylor finished, lifted her glass of tea, and sat back.

"Thank you, Aunt Veronica. I guess you're right. Obviously, it's what my body needed, and I need to get in the habit of giving it what it asks for."

"That's what I'm countin' on, sister." With a sly smile, Aunt Veronica lifted the empty tray and put it on the floor next to the bed.

Taylor's cheeks burned despite no one being in the room to hear her aunt's dirty reference. She took another sip of sweet tea in attempt to cool off her burning face.

"I have to be at the Boom Boom Room in thirty minutes. One of my bartenders called in sick, so I need to go cover," said Aunt Veronica as she looked at her watch. "But you know me, I can't rest until I know you've eaten."

She looked at Aunt Veronica and, for the first time, noticed a silver heart-shaped locket hanging from her neck. Taylor watched her aunt work to get the necklace off with little success, so she motioned for Aunt Veronica to turn to allow her to help.

"I've never seen this before," said Taylor just as she unhooked the clasp.

"Never? I've had it since I moved out of Mama's house when I was sixteen. I never wear it out to the bar because I'm afraid to lose it. Open it."

Taylor carefully opened it. She studied the two happy, young faces that met her inside. Two children, a boy and girl, were embracing each other in a loving bear hug. The little girl was a few inches shorter than the boy. She proudly smiled wide in the photograph, her chin held high in obvious pride. Taylor smiled at the girl's missing two front teeth. The boy affectionately rested his head on top of the small girl's, giving the camera a calm yet sweet, closed-mouth smile.

"We were six and eight there."

Taylor looked up at her. Aunt Veronica's watery eyes were softly staring down at the locket in Taylor's hand. "Best big brother you'd ever wanna meet," Aunt Veronica whispered.

For as long as she could remember, her aunt was always so bubbly and always ready to party. Yet, Veronica never seemed willing to break down her emotional walls with men, choosing to focus on Mr. Right Now rather than Mr. Right. But when it came to Taylor and her late father, Veronica's walls collapsed. Taylor knew her aunt loved her deeply, always commenting on how she looked like her daddy with the same smile and dimples, and how they shared the same quiet, effortless charm without demanding attention.

"Well, judging from that smile you're giving the camera, it looks like you were very aware of that, even at that age."

"How could I not be?" Veronica pointed a French-manicured finger at the photo. "Your daddy was about this age when Mama began her battle with depression. When Papa wasn't out chasing women, or passed out in his own puke on the front porch, he spent all his free time gambling our rent money away at the local game room. But with his temper, none of us minded him being gone all that much." Taylor could see the pain cross her dear aunt's face as she continued. "It was just a matter of months for Mama to go from bad to worse, and I remember her spending days, sometimes weeks, in bed. Joey took on the duties of dressing me for school every morning, styling my hair the best way a boy could, making my packed lunch, and cooking dinner when we got home from school. And every morning, he greeted his baby sister with a smile and hug.

"I still remember coming home from school about a year after this, the first day of the first grade. I came to him crying because all the children in my class had handwritten notes from their mamas tucked in their lunch sacks. I remember the agony that had crossed his face as I sat at the dinner table, crying hysterically, convinced I wasn't worthy of that kind of love. I thought maybe I had been a bad girl and that it was my fault Mama didn't write me letters. From that day on, I would find a note from Joey in my lunch sack every day."

Taylor quickly brushed away the tears that gathered on her lower lashes. "So Daddy was always Daddy, even at eight."

"Baby girl, look at me." Veronica held Taylor's chin in her fingers. "Your daddy will always be your daddy, and you will always be his baby princess. No one can ever take that away from you.." Taylor lowered her face as she fought the tears continuing to build in the back of her eyes, but Veronica only lifted her chin again. "You loved your daddy so much, baby, and, my God, did he love you. When they brought you home from the hospital, your mama would have to bribe him with steaks just to get him to hand you over." They both laughed at the image of her daddy, standing tall and macho in his dirty work clothes as he gently rocked a baby in his arms.

"I know it hurts, Taylor," Aunt Veronica continued. "Watching you grow up from a loving, affectionate child to an emotionally guarded young woman is not something your father would have wanted for you. You can't avoid love just to avoid the loss. That's not living, baby girl."

* * * *

Jay didn't feel his mind was in the present. As he carefully combed his freshly washed hair, he was actually debating about tomorrow. He wanted Taylor more than anything. After spending time with her over the week, his feelings had grown dangerously deeper. He couldn't imagine how much control he was about to lose the more he spent time with her.

To Jay, Taylor embodied all that he had been avoiding. She had class, beauty, brains, and a huge heart. A wife. A future mother.

Papa Craig poked his head in the bathroom, a wide smile spread across his face. He was wearing his favorite flannel robe and holding his nightly Southern Comfort on the rocks. "Hey, bubba, it's getting pretty late. You better make sure you're rested for your day with little Miss Taylor Ewing tomorrow."

"Yeah, Pops, just getting ready for bed, is all."

His father let out another whistle just as he had when he first saw Mrs. Bartlett's new Bugatti. "She sure is a peach if I ever saw one."

"Yeah, she even tastes like a peach."

Papa Craig threw his head back in a roar of laughter at Jay's instant response. Jay softly smiled at the nostalgically melodious sound. He always knew just what to say to make his father laugh like that.

"Well, my boy," Papa Craig wiped a laughing tear from under his glasses, "on that note, I'll see you in the morning." Papa Craig gave him a soft pat on his back and began turning to walk away.

"Pops?"

"Yeah, bubba?" No matter how old or successful Jay got, his father always spoke to him in the same soft and nurturing voice like he had when Jay was a toddler.

Jay took a second to choose his words carefully. "If you could do it all over again, with all the pain you feel now, would you still have shared a marriage with Papa Clark?"

"I'd gladly feel this pain for a thousand lifetimes just to relive those fifteen years again." His father said it casually, without hesitation, and walked away whistling.

Chapter 6

Honk! Honk, honk!

Taylor was dreaming she was in a floating basket, flying through the heavenly clouds as a band marched alongside her, the large group playing a song especially for her. And how appropriate, they were playing Bill Withers!

Honk, honk!

When she looked down, the basket began to slowly transform into…*Furby?*

As Taylor rolled in her bed, slowly coming to, her eyes struggling to open against the bright sunshine peering through the window, she realized the honking horn and the music was not from her dream, but from outside the house.

As she groggily sat up in her bed, she looked to her right at the alarm clock sitting on the side table. Eight a.m.

Before she could curse at whatever crazy bastard was being so rude, Aunt Veronica burst through the door.

"Aaah!" Taylor screamed and just about jumped out of her skin.

"Oh! My! *God!* Baby girl, you better look outside."

"Outside?" Taylor jumped out of bed then quickly pulled on her sleeping shorts. She ran to the front room and peered through the blinds. "What the—" There in the street, right in front of the house, were Brody and Jay standing up through the sunroof of a stretch Hummer, followed by the Male Order High School marching band enthusiastically playing "Lovely Day."

Taylor opened the front door and stood on the porch to get a better look. She noticed several neighbors were standing on their porches in their robes, happily dancing to the musical wakeup. Out in the yard, Aunt Veronica danced with the thirty-something bachelor from down the street. *Wow, so not only is it a ménage town, but it's full of crazy morning people, too?*

Taylor couldn't help but smile as she watched Jay and Brody being silly, dancing through the sunroof like a couple of drunken prom dates. The three teenaged drum majors that led the band were incredibly impressive, bending back low to the ground, coming back up in a high step, their batons flying high in the air then getting caught from behind. The band continued their march around the limo and down the street. When they rounded the corner, the music slowly fading with distance, the whole block broke out in applause and whistles. Taylor held back the giddy tears that were trying to break through her lashes, and her face was already hurting from smiling and laughing so much.

"That was incredible!" Taylor ran out to meet her men, barely noticing she forgot to grab a decent robe on the way out of the house. "I can't believe you set that up for me."

Jay shrugged. "Give a high school kid a hundred-dollar bill, and they'll do just about anything."

"Yeah, they were more than happy to wake up early for the surprise," Brody confirmed.

"But we're not done, so go get dressed. But thanks for returning the favor with your own show, princess." Jay indicated the sheer T-shirt she was wearing and gave her a devilish wink.

Looking down at herself, heat rushed to her face, and she immediately covered her erect nipples with her arms. Without another word, she ran in the house as she heard Brody and Jay laugh behind her.

* * * *

"Hmm, twenty minutes, pretty impressive." Brody looked up from his watch, and he stopped breathing. He stared at his Juliet making her way down the porch steps. He gave her an onceover from her red toe nails to her dazzling smile. She wore brown leather platform sandals, a light pink ruffled mini-skirt, and a khaki short-sleeved button-down that she tied above her naval, a hint of cleavage peaking from the several unfastened buttons on top. She wore several gold bracelets, and a small purse hung across her body. Even dressed casually, she was every bit the Dallas beauty queen.

"Well, sharing a community shower with twenty other freshmen had its benefits. You learn speed."

"Sounds brutal." Brody reached out to quickly brush his fingertips across the soft, exposed skin of the side of her waist. "Sorry, I couldn't help myself," he explained when she appeared to shudder from the touch.

She stared at him for a moment. "It's, um, it's okay. Just a little ticklish, is all."

"We'll try to keep that in mind," Jay told her as he took a step toward her. Brody could see Taylor's body stiffen when Jay closed the small distance between them. He then watched as their lips met, Jay's tongue slowly creeping through Taylor's mouth in a long kiss.

"Good morning, baby," Jay said softly, gazing in her eyes after breaking their kiss.

"Good morning." Taylor sounded breathless.

Jay broke her trance with a soft pat on her round ass as he gently nudged her to the limo. "Come on, let's get in. We have a long day ahead."

Once they were all settled in the back, Brody opened a bottle of Cristal to make a few mimosas. "Pulp or no pulp?" He held two different cartons of orange juice in front of Taylor.

"Pulp, please."

"You know, you're a little more country than we thought," Jay teased. "We just might end up overlooking the fact you grew up in the city."

"Well, Dallas city girls are pretty much country girls, but with better outfits." The men laughed at her joke.

"So now what?" Taylor asked as they drank from their champagne flutes.

"Well, we actually have a favor to ask." Brody carefully set down his glass on the surface next to the ice bucket. "The annual Male Order cotillion is in a few days, and we would love it if you were our date. That is, unless someone else has beat us to it." Brody silently wished they would have met her a little sooner. A girl like Taylor couldn't have gone this long in Male Order without at least a few date proposals.

"A few of the town boys have mentioned it, but to be honest, I don't have anything remotely appropriate to wear at such a grand ball, so I've just been declining the invitations."

"Just say yes, and we can take care of that right now." Jay might have attempted to hide the hope in his voice, but Brody knew his best friend enough to hear its underlying tone.

"As in you would *buy* me a dress?" Her eyes were wide in confusion. "That's incredibly sweet of you, but I just couldn't accept something like that." She pulled out her iPhone from her Marc Jacob's purse. "I have an extremely talented friend named Nikki back in Dallas who's been designing my gowns since we were kids. It's too short of a notice to have her design one now, but she always has several ready-to-wear pieces in her studio."

Taylor was cut off when Brody took the glass and phone from her hands then took them in his. He took a deep breath as he tried to repress the anger that was spreading within him. Her cheating ex, Dillon Day, obviously wasn't broke. The fact he never attempted to give his best to Taylor just confirmed how much of a tool he really was. No woman should feel guilty about being spoiled, especially one like Taylor. "Look, it's just one gown. Do this for us, and we promise you'll have a great time."

She hesitated for a moment before nodding. "Fine, but nothing too extravagant, okay?"

"Yeah, sure, whatever you say, princess." Jay pulled her face to his, kissing her while he eagerly undid the last few buttons of her shirt.

* * * *

It didn't seem like he could unbutton her blouse fast enough. The hitched sound of her breathing urged him to get to her tits faster. Jay breathed a heavy sigh of satisfaction when he finally felt a mound of warm, womanly flesh weigh heavy in his left hand.

The soft purr that escaped from Taylor's lips compelled him to lean down and take her sweet, pebbled beads in his mouth. He then removed his shirt and knelt between her open legs. He wanted to feel her warm cunt against his skin. He lightly sucked each nipple in turn while Taylor brushed her tiny fingers through his hair. Her moans had him looking up to view her beautifully flushed face. His erection grew painfully hard as he watched her bite her lower lip, her eyes closed as if she were straining to hold back her sounds.

Jay could feel the heat of her mound pressed against his chest while he rested snuggly between her thighs. The material of her panties grew damp against his skin, and he instinctively pressed his body closer to hers as the desire to make her scream morphed into a need. Taylor's body immediately reacted, and she bucked her hips against his hard pecs as if seeking further stimulation.

"Brody, come help me. Let's show our princess what it's like to be finger-fucked by two men at once." Taylor looked down to meet his gaze, her eyes widened in shock. Her gaze kept darting above their heads, obviously concerned with the driver knowing what dirty things they were doing in the backseat. But she didn't protest when Brody scooted over to them and joined Jay in massaging her inner thighs.

Her tits looked so damn delectable as they heaved with each breath she took, her need obviously growing as their hands inched closer to her waiting cunt. Taylor stared at their moving hands as they met at the v between her shivering thighs.

"Oh, baby, I can smell your sweet desire. You are *dripping* wet for us." Brody's impatience had him taking over as he pulled her lavender lace panties down past her knees and off her feet.

Jay spread her knees farther apart and looked down at Taylor's shaven pussy, licking his lips as he stared at his breakfast. "It's glistening with your juices, baby." Brody continued to stare transfixed on her naked bottom half.

"Fuck, I can see her pussy hole contracting with need already. It's begging to be stuffed with a long, giant dick, isn't it, princess?" Jay twirled a single index finger around her sopping entrance. He smiled as Taylor bucked her hips. He knew she hoped his finger would somehow slide straight into her oiled cunt.

* * * *

Taylor watched hungrily as Brody placed a single finger in his mouth and then let it join Jay's as it wedged between her engorged pussy lips.

"Lift your skirt up higher." Taylor didn't hesitate to follow Jay's insistent command. She lifted the ruffles of her skirt until the hem rested on her lower stomach, completely exposing herself in the sunrays that shone through the sun roof. Their eyes widened farther, encouraging Taylor to spread her pussy apart with her fingers to release her erect clit from its protective hood.

"Yeah, baby, you like playing with your pussy, don't you?" Brody's voice was seductive, but his smile remained gentle. "Did you finger-fuck yourself last night?"

"No," Taylor answered between heavy breaths. "I just pinched my clit over and over in front of my bedroom mirror until I came."

Both men growled at her description, and Taylor gasped loudly at the sudden intrusion of two fingers from two different hands in her cunt. Taylor's cries of arousal and the wet sound of her juices filled the limo as the two men wiggled their fingers all along her pussy walls, hitting every sweet spot inside of her. Her body heat rose, and her breaths became shorter and more erratic.

"Get completely naked, Taylor. Brody and I have something special for that puffy little nub down there just aching for attention."

Sounds good to me! Taylor quickly pulled off all her clothes and placed them in a messy pile on the seat next to her.

She watched as they both pulled down their pants and began to jerk off while they still had the index fingers of their left hands inside her pussy. Their beautiful cocks grew darker and longer with each tug. Their moans of passion pulled all the blood in her body straight down to her engorged pussy. She held her breath in anticipation for what they had planned for her.

"Harder, please," Taylor begged. Brody began to lightly circle her heated clit with a thumb, and Jay continued to pump his finger in and out of her.

"Spread yourself open really wide, then we'll give you your next surprise," Jay promised between heavy panting.

Taylor reached down with one hand and used her fingers to spread her lips open, but she needed so much more. "More, please! Please, Jay, I want my surprise!" Taylor pouted and cried out as she began to firmly pinch her own nipples with her free hand until she felt a dull pain send jolts of cream dripping from her folds and down the crack of her ass.

Just when Taylor felt the first sparks of an oncoming orgasm, Jay told Brody, "Now!"

Both men quickly moved in closer between her wide-open thighs, and each man placed their large, throbbing cocks firmly against either side of her desperate clit, using two rods of rock-hard steel to pinch the pink nub tightly. Both men cried out together as they completed their final jerks, and the violent pulses of their orgasms radiated through to Taylor's exposed clit.

Taylor could hardly believe her eyes. Both cocks throbbed against her exploding clit while two streams of hot, pearly white seed landed perfectly in the middle of her glistening abdomen. Taylor screamed her climax, yet she never took her eyes off the vibrating cocks that pressed down on her grateful hooded clit.

* * * *

After a delectable breakfast at Stephanie's of sweet potato biscuits with a bacon, goat cheese, and zucchini quiche, they strolled out into the SoMale shopping district.

"Wait, where's the limo?" She looked around at the parking spaces on the road, scanning the area for the shiny, long vehicle.

"I arranged for my truck to be waiting here for us so we can take a ride a little later to show you even more of the town," Jay replied as he and Brody each grabbed a hand and led her down the sidewalks of the large district.

Looking around, she realized she was surrounded by Chanel, Gucci, MAC, Marc Jacobs, and dozens of other designer boutiques. She smiled wide when she spotted "the food court," a cluster of five-star restaurants for the shoppers to enjoy during their day. Male Order seemed to be a girl's fantasy come true in every way.

"This is it," Jay said when they stopped in front of the glass doors of Jacqueline's. Taylor had never been inside the tall doors before, but she heard they had the most gorgeous dresses in Texas. When they walked into the boutique, Taylor realized that had been a complete understatement.

A flawlessly dressed woman greeted them when they stepped onto the black and white marble floor of the department store. "Welcome to Jacqueline's."

Immediately in front of them was the makeup counters, each having a friendly face to greet them as they passed by.

Jay grabbed Taylor's hand and led her to the woman, "Miss Ewing is giving us the pleasure of being our date to the cotillion this weekend, and she needs a dress."

The woman turned her bright smile to Taylor. "Follow me, please." She led them up a flight of stairs toward women's formalwear. It looked like a huge cathedral, only with mannequins draped in chiffon to worship. "I'm Ms. Roberts, and I will be assisting you today. Is there anything in particular you had in mind, my dear?"

Taylor looked around and immediately recognized some of the gowns. Paris fashion week was just the week before, and many of the dresses that were on the catwalk hung just a few feet away from her.

"Something simple," Taylor quickly responded before the men had a chance to answer.

The men both laughed, obviously knowing how modest Taylor was trying to be.

"Baby, nothing about you is simple," Brody said. "Just let Ms. Roberts show you a few things. And we've arranged for someone to come and help, so they should be here soon."

Taylor wasn't very comfortable at the thought of another man buying her something so elegant and just to wear once. In fact, the only gift she had ever received from a guy was a white and red teddy bear holding a box of chocolates that Dillon rushed to pick up from the drugstore for Valentine's Day.

Although she thought she had grown up in the high society of Dallas the last twelve years, the Male Order billionaire lifestyle trumped any flavor of luxury she had ever tasted. She used to get giddy when her step-father would buy her five hundred dollar BCBG dresses. But the gowns in Jacqueline's were McQueens and

Givenchys and...*sigh*...Dolces, dresses that had to be worth thousands!

"Okay, so did you want me to call you once I've found something?"

"What do you mean?" Brody looked confused.

"I mean, don't you two want to go kill some time while I try on clothes?"

"Are you kidding?" Jay replied, sitting on the snow-white quilted chaise that sat in front of the dressing room. "We're sitting right here. We wouldn't miss you trying on a bunch of sexy dresses for anything."

Taylor couldn't help but smile as Brody joined him in the white chair next to the sofa. It was like she had her own fashion catwalk and audience.

Ms. Roberts brought her dress after dress for her to model for her cotillion dates. But despite the obvious hunger in the gazes as they looked her over in each one, they always had the same response. "It's beautiful, but it's not the one." At first Taylor thought their honest opinions were refreshing. But after trying on the twelfth dress without success, she began to get frustrated. She couldn't help but to narrow her gaze at them when they still shook their heads no. Taylor turned to return back to the dressing room when Brody's voice stopped her.

"Oh, yes," Brody called out, "and here's our special guest now."

"*Good morning.* So sorry I'm late. Lip gloss crisis, my dears. And airport security, ugh! You understand, don't you, honey?"

Taylor's jaw dropped in shock. She couldn't believe her eyes when she turned toward the loud, flamboyant voice coming through the entryway. Skipping his petite frame over to Taylor, smiling brightly, wearing black head-to-toe except for the sequin raspberry beret on his head, was Jeremiah Giordano, last season's winner of *Mission: Vogue*. It was Taylor's favorite reality show, and she'd tuned in to the fashion competition every Sunday since season one.

Jeremiah had been the underdog of the season, a small-town Texas boy from outside of Houston with no formal fashion training. He went on to blow the judges away with his immaculate, fifteen-piece formalwear collection during the season finale. He had since transformed into one of the most in-demand couture designers in the entire world.

Taylor vaguely remembered mentioning *Mission: Vogue* being her favorite show when they were eating at Hester's the other day. But how were they able to get him here such short notice?

When Taylor didn't answer, speechless from the shock, Jeremiah added, "Oh, how adorable. She's shy! No worries, my dear, I'm going to design you the best gown this town has ever seen!"

Taylor turned to Jay and Brody, both smiling excitedly. "Wait, you mean I'm getting a custom-made evening gown?"

"We just decided to have a little fun with you to throw you off and make you think we were just going to buy one from the store," explained Brody proudly, then quickly assured her, "Don't worry about Ms. Roberts. We'll take care of her for her time. In fact, Jeremiah here is related to the Caldwells through his mother. The Caldwells have owned this store since Male Order was founded, so that gave Jeremiah the power to help us with our surprise."

The entire scene seemed so surreal, like a dream. "How much does that *cost*? You promised nothing too extravagant!"

Jay smirked. "Actually, we didn't promise anything, darlin'. Now just relax, and let us have our fun."

"So it's *fun* to spend an insane amount of money on a date's dress?"

"No," Brody answered, his face turning slightly serious. "It's fun to do anything it takes to make *you* smile."

Brody was gazing at her affectionately, bringing a warmth to her insides and, of course, a smile to her face. He smiled back and gave her a sweet wink. Then that heat spread down, immediately causing her clit to engorge with sensation. *Such a Prince Charming.*

Jeremiah stepped back to give her an onceover. "Wow, girl, look at you. Your boy toys mentioned on the phone that they had a beautiful Texas pageant queen they wanted to spoil, but, honey, you are one hot bitch!"

"Why, thank you." Taylor blushed at the compliment, still somewhat star-struck that the fashion industry's upcoming superstar of fierce was standing right there in front of her. She could hardly believe her five foot four frame would even be noticed by someone surrounded by flawless, six-foot-forever runway models.

"Okay, well to start off, I've brought a few sketches of ideas and some basic silhouettes you can try on so we can see what works best with your figure. Now I based these on what I saw of you on the Miss Dallas Texas Yellow Rose Web site, and your contestant profile mentioned your basic measurements, as well…"

* * * *

There it was. That killer smile. Her eyes sparkled when she smiled, like they were shimmering with the kindness that radiated from her heart. At breakfast, Taylor had told them more about her charity and all the events she single-handedly organized to raise money. Brody and Jay were already filled in by their mothers about how her father had passed when she was a child.

Brody had never imagined such a gorgeous woman could be so down to earth. She had a genuine motive to help others, and her passion for giving radiated through her excited little face when she spoke of all the upcoming projects the foundation was planning. He was impressed with how much time she devoted, how she felt compelled to protect others from the pain she felt from losing her father.

But the best thing about Taylor so far was how her face changed when their eyes would meet. She made him feel like a worshipped

God with the way she looked at him, just as crazy for him as he was for her.

Brody watched Taylor chat giddily with Jeremiah. She was affectionate by nature, he noticed. Taylor had a way of making Brody feel as though he were the only one in the room she could see and the only one who mattered. He saw now that she had woven her spell around Jeremiah as well. As they talked, she gazed into his eyes with her full attention, and she had a way of casually touching his arm when she wanted to emphasize a point. And, since they seemed to get along so well, Jeremiah continually brought out that intoxicating laugh of hers. He was rewarded as she took his hand and held it tightly for support while she hung her head back in a hearty laughter.

She and Jeremiah looked like old friends, sharing stories and going over silly fashion details. *She looks like an enraptured bride*, Brody thought, lost in his thoughts.

"So do you have a color preference for me?" Taylor's voice and face were painted in joy and excitement.

"Red," Jay replied without hesitation.

Taylor laughed. "I think that might be a bit of a fashion faux pas since my hair is dark auburn. Maybe hot magenta would be more chic?"

"First of all," Jay began, "I don't even know what hot magenta is. Second of all, I have no idea what is chic or what is faux pas in women's fashion."

Brody laughed and shook his head. He was thinking the exact same thing.

Jay's eyes lowered down her body, then back up her face, and then he said in a low voice, "But I do know that red on your toes heats me up enough to make me wonder what my reaction would be if that body of yours was draped in it."

Jeremiah gasped with a small hand covering his chest. "Oh, my."

Taylor smiled wide and turned to Jeremiah. "Red it is."

Jeremiah gave his head a small shake and broke his stare from Jay's body to turn to Taylor. "Oh, yes, well, we could do a deep, crimson-burgundy and use a pared down smoky eye and emphasize the lashes, then the glam-squad will balance the reds with a soft lip. I think it will be absolutely ravishing."

Taylor started to do a little jump and hop, softly clapping her hands as she visibly strained to keep herself from exploding with excitement. "My very own Jeremiah Giordano gown. I can't believe it!"

* * * *

Taylor felt like she stepped into a fairy tale. She tried on every sample gowns Jeremiah brought, allowing him to get a visual of her body in the different shapes. What she really loved was the look in the men's eyes when she came out in each dress. They looked at her like she was a goddess, like they were memorizing every contour of her face and every curve of her body. No crown or sash could ever make her feel that beautiful.

"Ok, you got one more. This one has an asymmetrical, strapless neckline, and it has lots of draping. I think something like this would emphasize that pretty little rack of yours." Jeremiah giggled as he gave her the last dress.

All these compliments were really making her blush. And she could hear it *all day*.

Taylor walked into the dressing room and stripped down to her lavender lingerie. Jeremiah gave a small knock on the door.

"Come in."

Only it wasn't Jeremiah.

Taylor gasped. "What are you doing? You can't be in here. They can kick us out if they see you in here!"

Brody smirked. "Baby, we can do what we want. The owners are very close friends to my family." He immediately began to undo his belt buckle casually as if he were doing nothing more than taking off a coat.

Taylor turned to Jay for help, but before she knew it, his hands were firmly holding her shoulders, pushing her to the floor on her knees in a single swift move. "I get hard just knowing I put that smile on your pretty face."

She looked up at the men and said, "Let me see what I can do about putting one on your faces, too."

By the time Brody had his giant erection pointed at her cheek, Jay was fishing out his own monster length.

There she was, near naked with two huge cocks twitching in anticipation for her watering mouth. Taking each hot erection in her hands, they all three groaned at the warm contact. Their large cocks felt like velvet-covered steel, their masculine scent causing her moisture to gather at the small lace patch covering her mound. Suddenly, she couldn't give a rat's ass who was outside the door.

Taylor looked up in their eyes and unclasped her bra. At once, each had a large hand covering her tits, and both men furiously tweaked the sensitive, hardened nubs, causing her to whimper with pleasure.

She pulled both of their cocks to her mouth, slowly swirling the heads with her tongue in a figure-eight motion, over the top of Brody's, down to scrape the underside of Jay's, circling to run it around and across the top of Jay's, then down to scrape the underside of Brody's. Four hands came up to grasp her hair as a low, double groan reached her ears.

She took each in her mouth one at a time, swallowing around them to get them nice and wet while she deep-throated them ravenously. Once they were glistening with her spit, she started to alternate jerking-off one while sucking down the other.

Their hips bucked as they silently begged for more of her mouth. Their hands were going back and forth from squeezing her hard nipples to grabbing the back of her head for deeper penetration.

"Open your mouth for us, sugar." Jay was panting his response, seemingly close to completion.

Taylor opened her mouth wide with her tongue sticking out while they both began to eagerly tug their throbbing, purple-tinted dicks. When she reached up and began to gently pull and fondle their balls, they each grabbed one of her shoulders, brought their cocks closer to her open mouth, and moaned huskily as two pearly-white, hot streams began to shoot in her mouth. Taylor did her best to swallow every drop, but a few drops landed on her naked breasts.

Both men leaned back against the dressing room wall, and their eyes closed as they struggled to regulate their breathing.

Another knock on the door.

"All right, bitches, y'all had y'all's fun. I'm sure Miss Thang has had her daily dose of man protein. Now come out before we all get hungry for some meat!" Jeremiah broke out in giggles. Then his sweet southern voice suddenly turning sassy, and he snapped, "And don't let me see any stains on those gowns, or I'm taking a switch to those perky bottoms!"

* * * *

It was almost seven o'clock when they finally walked outside to the warm, breezy evening air. It reminded Jay of Sunday nights as a boy when the maids would routinely wash and iron the bed sheets for the week. The feel of the crisp, cool sheets would immediately relax him to sleep.

As they walked back to the truck, Jay inhaled deeply, the aroma of the fresh blossoms that surrounded them, making him think of only one thing. He'd been eight years old when his parents celebrated their tenth anniversary. His fathers chose to slave for almost a year prior to create his mother's dream secret garden.

When Mama had seen how hard they had to work in order to complete the garden as a two-man team, she urged them to hire help, for their sake. Papa Craig and Papa Clark had refused the help, hell-bent on doing the project themselves. They wanted Mama to know this garden was completely built by her husbands' own four hands.

Mama loved that garden. It was her "personal slice of heaven," as she used to say. It became an escape from the world for not only his parents, but also for Jay throughout his childhood and teen years. When he was shut in by the mystical stone walls of the secret garden, he felt like he was shut out of the world of teen angst and misunderstanding adults and into a world of Zen and nirvana.

He knew Papa Craig and his mama were still sticklers about the upkeep of the garden, but since his Papa Clark's death, Jay hadn't been able to bring himself to open the door in the stone wall that led to the confined paradise.

As he walked beside Taylor, watching her eyes sparkle with childlike joy as she giggled at Brody's boyish charm and jokes, Jay wanted nothing more than to see that joy on Taylor's face for the rest of his life.

The rest of my life? Yes, the rest of my life. If I let her get away, it won't be long before she finds a guy smart enough to know she is a miracle to treasure and to take care of.

The thought of another man besides him and Brody touching her, stealing her heart, making a family with her made Jay curl his hands into fists. His nails were beginning to break his skin when he realized what he was doing, so he took a deep breath to calm his red-hot temper. *Fuck this macho, playboy bullshit. I can't fucking lose her.*

As Jay slid into the truck seat, Taylor to his right and Brody to hers, he interrupted Taylor and Brody's conversation. "Change in plans. Taylor, we're taking you to another surprise location." Brody immediately shot Jay a confused look but stayed silent.

"Another surprise!" exclaimed Taylor, her eyes wide with anticipation. "Well, if it's as breathtaking as the last surprise—"

"More so," interrupted Jay, turning to give Taylor a smile. She gave him a wide grin in response, her eyes now sparkling with anticipation. Looking over at his friend, he could tell from Brody's now shocked face that he had a pretty good idea about where they were heading.

* * * *

It began to lightly rain outside as the rode down the neighborhood roads of Male Order. They were headed toward Jay's house, passing by Aunt Veronica's and blocks of other family houses. Brody could feel Taylor gently sway in place to the beat of the radio, a soft song coming from under her breath, her full pink lips pursed in a whistle when she didn't know a lyric. The shape they made had Brody wishing he could bury his cock between those sweet lips.

Suddenly, just as they were about to pull up to Jay's house, the song "God Blessed Texas" came on the radio, and Taylor gasped loudly in excitement. "Oh, my God! I *love* this song!" she exclaimed, jumping up and down in her seat. "Turn it up, and pull over, pull over!"

"Taylor, you're going to get soaked," said Brody as he gently placed his hands on her thigh. But the song must have peaked Jay's curiosity. He quickly pulled over to the side of the dirt road to see just what she had planned.

When the truck came to a stop, Taylor turned up the music louder, and then she quickly crawled over him and out of the car. The truck's headlights shone directly on Taylor's petite form as she made her way to the front of the truck, the misty rain already slightly dampening her mini skirt, the thin material clinging to the luscious curves of her tight, curvy body.

* * * *

God blessed Texas with His own hand
Brought down angels from the Promised Land....

Even though she was blinded by the headlights, Taylor could feel the two pairs of gorgeous eyes staring at her through the windshield. She normally danced only in dark, crowded clubs, but the carefree child buried inside her was once again summoned when she heard the first few notes of the familiar country tune. When she had jumped out of the truck, she hadn't intended to give her little audience a striptease. But it was as if a cloud of magic potion trailed Jay and Brody, spreading a dust of crazy through her senses.

As she swayed her hips and popped her ass, she felt that magic potion spread through her consciousness, relinquishing her inhibitions. Again, she imagined the magic had kidnapped the self-conscious, cynical beauty queen that arrived from Dallas and delivered a woman without a fear in the world. Not even the possibility of Jay and Brody hurting her was enough to break through the magic shield. She knew just one night of pleasure with the billionaire gods would be worth nine lifetimes of pain.

* * * *

Taylor's sultry dark gaze never left their direction as she began to dance seductively. Turning to the side, dipping her ass low, then slowly bringing it up, her back arched like a sex kitten, she then gave a playful little slap to her wet ass. Jay and Brody growled in lust at the same time at the sight of water splashing out from the wet contact made between her petite hand and round ass.

Brody's cock quickly grew warm and hard as he watched the thin material of her skirt cling to the curves of her body as more of the night rain saturated her clothing. Everything on her body, the rounded bottoms of her breasts, her perky, pebbled nipples, her ass as it bounced to the beat, all looked as though they were painted in the wet material of her outfit. Her wet skirt dipped between her legs to cling to her inner thighs and the V of her perfectly shaped pussy.

"This is not happening right now," Brody said under heavy breath, wiping the sweat from his forehead with the back of his hand as his arousal increased with each pounding of the beat. "Ugh, *dear God*, tits that perfectly round should be a sin."

"You know, I used to hate this song as a kid," Jay said as he reached in his pants. "But now," he breathed heavily as he began to tug, "I'll never be able to hear it without comin' on myself."

Brody's attention was back on the tiny dancer, and his dick began to pulsate as Taylor swayed to the beat. She snaked her arms above her head, her breasts teasing him as they threatened to pop out the unbuttoned blouse. Taylor slowly and slightly dipped down at the knees, facing the men, then straightened with one hip cocked, dipped again, then came up with the other hip cocked. She stared at them like she knew exactly what she was doing to them, occasionally giving them a full smile, her eyes sparkling as her face would turn from seductress to innocent sprite. Taylor's cinnamon-brown hair hung in wet twists, her bangs limp with water as they grazed over her eyebrows, partially hiding her rich puppy dog eyes.

Sure, Brody'd had his share of "private dances." They usually consisted of awkward hip and ass jerks, sloppy lip licks, too much bourbon, and cheesy props like feather boas or a pole bought from a wacky adult gift shop, but hey, they had tried their best. Bless their relentless souls, those other women had absolutely nothing on the fresh, twirling princess glowing in the headlights before them.

Other girls had dressed in tacky lingerie and had no expression on their faces as they concentrated on the moves they learned in the aerobic striptease classes at their gyms. But Taylor's body moved with proud joy as she let the music guide her movements, not a hint of self-consciousness apparent in her rocking hips. Her only props were the headlights and the rain, both saturating her from her long, chocolate-cherry hair to her cherry toe nails.

* * * *

Jay only took his eyes off of the dancing beauty for just a second to glance at Brody and say, "I have to have her, Brody. *All* of her." He smiled, a liberating feeling washing over him as Brody responded with an eager smile of his own, his eyes swimming with delight. Jay turned his attention back to the tanned goddess, now wantonly rolling her torso to the beat as she combed the front of her rain-drenched hair back with those perfectly manicured, tiny fingers, her breasts rising and falling with the slow waves that ran from her hips to her torso, then releasing through her chest.

Well, I've been sent to spread the message
God blessed Texas…

Taylor began to slowly make her way to the driver's side window, still slightly swaying as the song began to wrap up. Brody rushed to slide across the seat, ignoring the pained grunt coming from his friend as he supported his weight on the palm resting on Jay's thigh. In one swift movement, Brody wiped a clean streak through the steam that had collected on Jay's window. Taylor now stood right in front of the driver's window, looking at Jay and Brody with a whimsical smile on her face like she hadn't just given them, and their pulsating cocks, the most erotic show of their existence.

Taylor then began to slowly unbutton the last few buttons of her shirt. She pulled the sides of the shirt from her chest to reveal the light purple bra underneath. Jay's breath caught in the back of his throat when he realized he could see her dark pink, pebbled nipples right through the sheer lace.

Taylor let her head fall back, face up in the falling rain, as she pressed her lush tits against the window, the glass spreading her breasts into enormous, lace-covered globes. Jay and Brody pushed their faces against the window like two puppy dogs at a pet shop begging for a warm, cozy home, but Jay's only concern was to get as close as possible to their Taylor, *their* Taylor, the angel-faced minx who had haunted his dreams since the moment he saw her.

Taylor continued to pull down her shirt, moving painfully slow in a tormenting game, giving the men an amused cock of a perfectly shaped eyebrow. She allowed the shirt to fall then worked on her skirt. When it fell to her feet, she was left standing in her lavender lace bra and coordinating panties.

"I've never hated purple lace so much before. Just gets in the way," said Jay with his nose pressed against the glass as he hungered for the perfectly waxed pussy that peeked through the sheer lace like a decadent dessert seducing passersby to come into a bakery. And Jay could only imagine how succulent and moist that dessert tasted.

Taylor closed her eyes and kissed the window twice, leaving two pink lip shapes on the wet tinted glass.

Jay gripped his dick a little tighter and pumped his length slowly, just enough to relieve the ache but not too much to send him over the brink. He looked over and saw Brody's hand was slowly pumping in his pants, as well, his stare never leaving Taylor. Brody breathed heavy and deep, still managing to say, "Well, my man, looks like we found ourselves a bride."

Chapter 7

The warm, humid summer rain felt sinful as it ran down Taylor's body, soaking her lace bra and thong. She'd never felt so sexy as she watched Jay and Brody undress to pump their long, wide cocks while they raked her body up and down with their eyes.

When she leaned over and gave the window two pink kisses, she could hear their growls of frustration through the glass and saw their hands speed up their up-and-down motions. The ache in her channel had been going on for so long, her pussy walls were now contracting around emptiness. She didn't care if it had to be in a truck, she needed that emptiness filled right then.

She wrapped her fingers around the door handle, took a deep breath, then opened it. It was barely half opened when she felt two strong hands grip her waist and drag her in. In a flash, Jay had her laid across his and Brody's laps, her head in Brody's and her ass resting on Jay's huge, stiff erection.

Before she could speak, Brody's fingers tangled in the back of her hair as he pulled her mouth toward his, his tongue immediately pushing itself through her lips, sucking them in a ferocious hunger. Jay effortlessly lifted her body to his mouth, his strong hands squeezing her ass, and he began a trail of kisses and licks around her abdomen. A jolt of electric heat traveled from the areas he licked down to her soaking pussy. When she felt his tongue dip in her bellybutton, she flinched from the tickle.

Jay laughed softly, making a husky sound from the back of his throat. "You taste like a honey-drizzled peach."

"Mmm." Taylor moaned at Jay's words, rolling her hips in a circular motion as his pointed tongue softly swept across her skin.

Brody's kiss was now a little softer, and he was exploring every surface of her mouth. His tongue retreated, and he began to trace the edges of her lips as he barely brushed them with his. She could smell his sweet shampoo mixed with the clean, masculine sweat that glazed his tanned skin. It reminded her of the time she and her best friend, Avery, a proud gay even at fourteen, snuck into the varsity boys' locker room after the team's two-a-day, hoping to get their first glance at the perfection that is a male athlete's naked body. They barely missed them by a few minutes, but Taylor could remember the rugged, clean smell that had still lingered in the warm steam of the shower room.

As Jay's tongue lavished attention on her lower stomach, Taylor raked her nails through his scalp, his feather-soft, dark hair caressing the webs of sensitive skin between her fingers like damp silk. He slowly lowered her ass down to his enormous hard-on as he trailed his gaze up and down her form. "I could come just looking at you." He wedged a single finger into the wet lace panties she still wore, and he slowly trailed the finger around the curve of her hip, descending down where it met the crease of her inner-thigh. Taylor squeezed her thighs together in shame when she felt his finger discover the erotic juice that was trickling down her thigh.

"Damn, baby, that's not just the rain that soaked your panties, is it?" Jay pushed her knees farther apart. "C'mon, baby girl, let us see it." He growled when she relaxed her trembling legs, allowing her mound to be on full display as he pulled the lace material down her hips. He threw the lace scrap to Brody who opened the glove compartment to place it inside.

"Wait, am I getting those back?"

"Not a chance," Brody whispered in her ear before capturing her sensitive lobe between his teeth, making her groan in lust. She wouldn't let Brody and Jay get away with stealing her panties, but now wasn't the time to sass either of them.

Brody moaned her name and forcefully pulled down the underwire of her strapless bra until it rested in the middle of her stomach. Her full breasts bounced out at the release of the confinement. Taylor arched up so she was able to reach behind her, unhook the bra, and throw it over Jay's head and onto the street pavement.

"Holy *fuck*," Brody groaned as he leaned down to take one of her breasts in his mouth, his hand capturing the other in a firm squeeze. He hummed around her nipple, causing Taylor to buck her hips up in response. His eyes were closed as if he were savoring the taste of her.

The deep warmth of Jay's palm rested on her folds, lightly moving in large circles. Her gut tightened as she wondered what his next move would be. And then he began a soft spanking against her aching slit, the slapping sound becoming louder as he increased the power little by little. "Even a perfect pussy like this needs to be taught a lesson every now and then. Gotta remind her who's boss."

The intensity of the pleasure shocked and aroused her. She'd never been spanked before, much less been spanked on her pussy, but wave after wave of warm tingles flooded her body with each slap, the chill spreading to the back of her neck and stealing her breath. His warm hand was so big it easily slapped against every exposed nerve of her cunt.

"Ohh, Jay and Brody," Taylor mumbled, and the sound of both of their names intensified the passion running through her body. "Mmm, Jay *and* Brody," she cried louder. Again she heard husky growls coming from both of the men at the same time, causing her cream to run down her slit and trickle down to lubricate her asshole.

Jay's erotic pussy spankings suddenly stopped, and he began to gently and slowly wipe two fingers over her lips and folds, brushing over every exposed inch of her mound while Brody's mouth continued sucking her nipples. Then he started a gentle tap over her throbbing clit with the pad of one of his fingertips, and Taylor's heavy sighs grew louder as her hips began a rhythmic bucking motion in coordination with the tormenting taps. The tapping was so gentle that her pussy ached with the need for more intense friction. Just when she was going to put aside her pride and beg him for more, Jay oiled two large, wide fingers with her abundant desire before inserting them into her hot pussy.

"Oh, yes. *Please.*" Taylor tried to squeeze her thigh muscles, attempting to stop the violent shudder, but it seemed they had a mind of their own. She decided to push aside the embarrassment of her eager response, and she allowed herself to enjoy the wiggling glide of Jay's fingers. Usually when guys in the past had tried to use their fingers on her, they were too eager and rough, and it brought more pain and annoyance than pleasure. But tonight, her pussy was so ready and so wet, Jay's fingers pumped her saturated channel with little effort.

Suddenly, Jay used a fingertip of his other hand to give her another electrifying clit tap while the fingers inside her continued to work her in a corkscrew motion. Taylor struggled to keep her breathing under control. She grabbed Brody's ears like a jockey holding a mare's reigns as he continued to lick currents of sexual shock into her body through her erect nipples and down to the muscles pulsating around Jay's fingers.

Without warning, the twisting sensation in her womb tightened with psychotic force, and her vision blurred. Her orgasm seemed to come from every part of her. Brody held her breasts together and nibbled her nipples at the same time, causing a violent jerk in her body as she shrieked their names with her completion.

"Damn, you have to feel how dripping wet she is for us," Jay said to Brody as he slowly withdrew his fingers once Taylor came back to Earth.

"Mmm, I intend to." Brody lightly sucked and licked the spot where her shoulder met her neck, then glided the soft tip of his nose along her jaw line until he met her lips in a soft kiss.

"Not until I'm done." Before Taylor could register Jay's words, he grabbed the sides of her ribs to sit her up, pulled her toward him, and placed her on his lap with her legs straddling his thighs as he sat behind the wheel. Brody released a disappointed groan as she was yanked from his lap.

Jay's eyes were glazed over with passion and lust as he brushed her disheveled, wet hair from her face. He grabbed the back of her neck and pulled her head down to devour her mouth with his. It seemed like her weight on his cock intensified his passion when he impatiently unzipped his pants to allow his hard-on more room.

As she continued to kiss Jay, Brody leaned over and continued licking the sensitive nape of her neck. She moaned softly as his hands slowly grazed down her back then eagerly palmed her ass.

She felt Jay fumbling to pull his pants lower as she continued to kiss him passionately and lovingly. Jay lifted her by the hips, and she suddenly felt the wide, blunt head of Jay's cock press against her entrance.

Brody interrupted them before Jay could push in. "Hold on." Jay and Taylor broke their kiss to look at Brody. "I want you to suck my cock as Jay fucks that hot pussy."

* * * *

Jay smiled up at Taylor when he saw her eyes grow heavy with lust at Brody's request.

Jay opened the truck door and gently lifted Taylor off his lap as he scooted to get out, leaving his gorgeous princess naked in the driver's seat. He felt the warm water trickle down his body as he stood in the evening rain. The opened door left the car light on, and Taylor looked even more beautiful as he was able to examine her body in the better light.

In a sudden, uncontrollable hunger, Jay grabbed Taylor's lush hips and turned her so she was bending over with her plump ass toward him. "Ohh," she whimpered when he gave her right ass cheek a loud spank. She seemed to be aroused from the contact as she wiggled her round ass against his erection in appreciation.

Brody began to quickly pull down his pants, and soon there were two enormous erections popped out on display. Jay watched as Taylor reached over to Brody, raking her nails through the hair at the base of his shaft, then wrapped her tiny hand around his pulsing dick. Brody sucked in a sharp breath at the contact. She then slowly licked him from his balls up to his glistening head. She moaned loudly when Jay grabbed his cock and began to tease her dripping slit. He ran the head back and forth over her pussy hole, spreading her cream everywhere.

When Taylor leaned down on her forearms, her ass lifting higher, she looked back and gave Jay a smile, then closed her eyes and bit her lower lip as she waited for his next move. No longer able to hold back, Jay pushed his cock all the way inside her channel. Taylor screamed at the stretch.

"Holy fuck! Oh my God, baby." Taylor felt so tight and hot, so smooth. "Are you okay, baby?"

"So…so…*big*," Taylor panted, her tiny body trembling as it took him in.

Jay wanted to pound her cunt right away, but he kept his control as he slowly moved in and out, allowing Taylor to get used to his size. After a few seconds, she began to meet his thrusts with her own, and Jay could see that her pain had receded. She gave him the silent go-ahead when she swung her head back, her long, auburn hair spread out against her naked back. He couldn't help himself, and he grabbed her hair with his right fist as he kept his left hand on her hip.

Three loud, moaning voices filled the air as Taylor then took Brody in her mouth. Brody's head fell back against the seat as he moaned her name in ecstasy. "Oh, Taylor, keep going, sugar. Suck that cock, baby. Yeah, you like the way my dick tastes, don't you?"

Brody's raunchy words seemed to intensify the lust in Taylor as her sucking noises grew louder and wetter, her round ass bouncing hard against Jay's body. Her tits swayed freely with their lovemaking, and he watched her delicate, manicured hand work its black magic on Brody's pulsating cock as she pumped in sync with her mouth.

Jay ran his hand down her soft back, meeting her feminine curves as he relished the magnetic pull of her body. For some reason, this woman had him more hypnotized than any conquest he ever had before. He couldn't decide if it was her flawless face, or her soft curves, or her hypnotic laugh, or the way her eyes softened at the sight of him. "Damn, look at you baby. You're so gorgeous, princess."

"You feel so good," Taylor said in her southern belle drawl. She sounded so sexy and sincere. Brody gently directed her head back down on his lap, and Jay could once again hear the eager sucking sounds of Taylor's mouth. Within seconds, Brody was clenching his fists in her hair, giving a loud groan and jerk as he filled her mouth with his cum. "Yummy," Taylor said as she licked the last of his cum from his glistening shaft. Brody was limp with exhaustion, his chest heaving as he struggled to regain his breath.

Jay's thrusts pounded quicker, harder, and Taylor whipped her head back as she joined him in the search for their carnal finish. As he felt his balls tighten for release, Jay bent over Taylor's soft form, his chest pressed down on her warm back. "Squeeze those delicious thighs for me, Taylor. Yeah, yeah, that's it. Damn, you're so tight." Taylor squealed her second climax of the night as the velvet walls of her pussy began to frantically contract around his rock-hard cock.

"So. Fucking. Beautiful. *Fuck*!" Jay pounded his torso against her quivering form with each word as his completion clouded his sight. His body quaked as his seed filled Taylor's body. He rested flat against her sweat-glistening flesh until his breath returned to normal.

He slowly pulled out of her and stood, the cool night drizzle refreshing his heated body. As he tucked himself back in his boxer-briefs, he watched Taylor gently put her hand on Brody's flushed cheek before giving him a soft, romantic kiss. They made a beautiful couple. A sharp ache formed in Jay's chest as he yearned to join them in their liberating state of love.

Taylor broke free of Brody's lips and looked over her shoulder at Jay. Another man-eating smile, another stab in Jay's chest. The love that was in her eyes when she had looked at Brody remained when she stared at Jay. It remained clear as day. *Holy shit, she's in love with me.*

Jay had to quickly turn his head from Taylor's angelic caramel eyes before he'd say something he'd regret. He swiftly turned away from the sight of her face and leaned against the car. He tightly squeezed his eyes shut to squash the dull pain stuck in his chest as he dropped his head back in the falling rain.

When he saw that devotion, that true love, in her eyes, it took everything in him not to fall to her lap and thank the dear Lord for her heart. He wanted to hold her and protect her and make sure she'd never go without that look again. But the image of Papa Clark and Mama dressed in black, holding each other as they sobbed in depression, haunted his thoughts.

You can't do this. Just hit it and quit it. Don't be a damn fool and give in like Brody's dumb ass has.

* * * *

Jay's eyes had softened and darkened to a pine color when he was staring at her face. He had parted his lips, and just when Taylor could have sworn he was about to say something, he had suddenly turned to look away from her. Taylor furrowed her brow. She just didn't understand it.

"Jay?" she whispered, her gut clenching in instinctive anxiety. She feared what excuse he would provide for his suddenly distant behavior.

"Get dressed." She hardly heard him, but the anger in his voice was like a bomb going off. When she turned to Brody, his puzzled look provided her no explanation for why Jay was acting so strange.

Jay turned back to them and leaned down to make direct eye contact with her. "Are you fucking deaf? I said get dressed!"

She grabbed her lace bra and scooted out of the truck, joining him in the empty road while she struggled to put her bra back on. She felt the warm tears start to stream down her face as reality crept up on her. She bent down to grab her wet skirt from the road. After stepping into it, she looked up into Jay's piercing jade eyes. She thought they looked misty, but he immediately turned his face away again before she could get a good look.

"Jay, if you think we might be moving too fast, m-maybe we can talk about it."

"There's nothing to talk about, Taylor!" Taylor flinched again at his sudden yelling. "There's nothing more going on here, don't you understand? Or are you that fucking *delusional*?"

Taylor covered her mouth as a gasp of horror escaped her throat. The salty tears wouldn't stop coming.

Brody was suddenly at their side, fastening his belt. "Hey, man, don't talk to her like that! She's a female, for Christ's sake."

"I can say whatever the *fuck* I want, Brody. Just because *you* think her pussy is good enough to give up your life doesn't mean *I* think it is, too."

That was it. Enough was enough. "You sunovabitch," Taylor mumbled between gritted teeth. "You shady douchebag. Don't you *ever* talk about me that way!" Her heat of her temper scorched within her as the reality of her heart shattering came into focus.

Jay took another step toward her. "What's wrong, darlin'? Not used to being told your cunt is mediocre at best?"

By reflex, Taylor shrieked, and her hand landed hard in a loud smack against Jay's face. "What the fuck has gotten into you? *Are you fucking crazy?*" Brody's fighting words were then followed by more yells, but Taylor was running farther down the country road, their curses fading behind her as she frantically moved to escape them.

How could she be so stupid? *Again!* They had used her. She thought they were falling in love with her, but she was nothing but a truck-stop receptacle to them, just something to relieve themselves in as they went on their way.

Taylor guessed she had been jogging south for at least half an hour before the Luscious salon sign came into sight. The closed sign was already hanging, but she could see the lights were still on, so it couldn't have been much past eight. She ran up the steps, swung open the door, slammed it shut, and dropped to the floor as she broke down into a hysterical crying fit.

"Good God! Veronica! Veronica, come quick!" Greta ran to Taylor's side and knelt down to her, pushing her drenched, disheveled hair out of her face.

"Oh my Lord! Baby girl, what happened to you?" Veronica dropped to the floor with them, grabbing Taylor's face as she evaluated her with terrified eyes. Beverly was jogging over with a cup of water as Aurora sat beside them and began to dab Taylor's face with a dry towel.

"Auntie Veronica," Taylor sobbed. "I ha-hate th-them." She could hardly speak. The waterfall of tears was stealing her breath.

Veronica gently pressed Taylor's head against her chest. "Shh, baby, shh." Veronica rocked her gently, but Taylor's sobs didn't slow down.

* * * *

"I'm sorry, Brody, but I can't do this. It's completely pointless. I promise you, it's for our own good!"

Brody's face was crimson with fury, and his chest heaved with shallow breaths as his fists hung stiffly at his sides. He looked like he was ready to rip someone's head off. He stepped up fearlessly until he was an inch from Jay's face.

"You just hurt the one woman we will ever love, you crazy piece of *shit*!" Brody closed his eyes for a second as if trying to calm himself down. In a more simmered tone, he continued, "If you fucked this up, Jay, I swear to God, I will never speak to you again. You'll be *dead* to me, and so will the last twenty years of our friendship. You have my word." Brody grabbed his shirt from the car then turned and began to jog in the direction Taylor had run.

Jay sunk down in the driver's seat. Heat rose to his face, and he began to punch the dashboard with his right fist. He didn't stop until a smear of blood appeared against the leather surface. But the pain in his heart was too distracting to feel the pain of his knuckles being split open.

Brody just didn't get it. He *had* to say those things. It didn't matter that he didn't mean a word of it. It became obvious that Taylor was in love with them both when she looked over her shoulder and gave him that loving stare. A woman like that wasn't going to give up her love easily, not unless he hurt her, not unless he broke her heart.

Something sparkly caught his peripheral vision. He turned and saw a tiny silver high-heeled sandal lying on the car floor. He had bought them for Taylor while they were at Jacqueline's after he caught her eyeing them several times during her fittings. He picked it up and stared at it. He imagined Taylor's cherry red toes sitting pretty in it, thought of when she had looked up from painting those toes to smile up at him and Brody that first day as they rode the four-wheelers in front of her house. Then he thought of her wearing that smile as she walked toward him down a long church isle, dressed in white.

The blood from the open wounds on his hand began to drip on the new metallic leather of the shoe.

"Shit. What have I done?"

Chapter 8

Brody breathed a sigh of relief when he came upon Aunt Veronica's house and saw a few lights were on. He glanced at his watch. He had been running south for over an hour and a half.

He quietly walked to the side of the house, careful to remain in the shadows of the bushes to keep from sight. And there she was.

Brody ducked down a little as he peered through Taylor's window. She was sitting at her vanity with her back toward him, but he could see her reflection in the mirror. Her eyes were puffy and red from crying, and her bottom lip slightly trembled as if she would break down again at any moment. She was brushing her wet hair, but her gaze seemed far away. She was wearing nothing but a pair of navy boy shorts and a Male Order High School football jersey that looked like it was from the eighties.

She stood, and still facing the mirror, she lifted the jersey just enough to slather some lotion of her flat stomach. Even from a distance, he could see her nipples had hardened against the jersey fabric, creating two perfect little peaks at the tips of her unconfined breasts. Brody had never seen anything more adorable.

He watched as Veronica opened Taylor's bedroom door and said something to her. He couldn't hear their conversation, but they exchanged a few words, then Veronica walked over, gave Taylor a nurturing hug, and kissed the top of her head. When Veronica walked out, Taylor went over to the lamp by the window, turned it off, and pulled down the shade.

Brody looked around the yard, making sure no one was hanging out on their porches to catch him in his pathetic act. After he was certain he was alone, he carefully crept up to her window and tapped it softly, hoping not to startle her. He saw the shade move to the side and a pair of large brown eyes stared straight at him.

Taylor pulled up the shade then the window. "What are you doing here, Brody?" she demanded. "Get out of here before I grab my auntie's shotgun and blow your head clean off."

"Taylor, I love you."

"What in God's name—"

"I do, I love you, Taylor Ewing. I've loved you since the moment I laid eyes on you."

Taylor narrowed her gaze at him. "Look, I don't know what you and your friend have been smoking, but ya'll are nothing but a couple of crazies, if you ask me."

In an instant, Brody was on his knees in the dewy grass. His dignity was the last thing that mattered to him at that moment, and he reached up and grabbed her hands in desperation. "Please, Taylor, just give me a moment to explain myself. Please." Hell must had frozen over because he was literally begging a woman for merely a chance to talk, but his need to win Taylor's heart back pushed away any pride he had left.

"Why, I never heard of such bad taste," she replied bitterly, a wave of her hand indicating his shameless slave position. Brody held his breath in anticipation as he watched Taylor exhale a frustrated sigh then look to her left and right for any onlookers.

"Well, hurry on in before you catch cold."

* * * *

The lamp fell to the floor in a loud crash as Brody's foot caught the bedside table. He fell to her bedroom floor with a heavy thud then sprung back on his feet in the blink of an eye. "I'm okay," he whispered. "Shake it off, shake it off," he mumbled to himself as he hopped from one foot to the other, apparently trying to ease his pain.

Taylor turned to hide the smile that threatened to peak the corners of her mouth.

Before she had the chance to turn back to face him, she felt his warm breath tickle the back of her neck as he ran his fingers lightly down the sides of her arms. "What do you want, Brody?" She tried her best to sound angry, but it was a little difficult when she had to speak in a whisper.

"Taylor, I—"

"Shh! Aunt Veronica is in the next room," she warned as she turned back to face him.

Lowering his voice, he continued, "I'm sorry about what happened tonight. I don't know what's gotten into Jay, but I'm skinning his hide the next chance I get for talkin' to you the way he did."

The mere mention of the man's name had hot tears blurring her vision before she could stop them. "I don't understand, Brody." She wiped the falling tears from her cheeks. "He was so cruel, so heartless to—"

Before she could finish her sentence, Brody had her mouth captured with his in a ravenous kiss. Suddenly, the pesky ill thoughts of Jay began to lift from her mind. She inhaled the grassy outdoor smell that had mixed with Brody's clean, masculine scent. She grabbed the back of his neck in need.

Brody lifted his shirt off, his body a glowing, chiseled masterpiece as the moonlight shone through her window, bathing him in a mystic silver glow. He was absolutely stunning, a true god in human form. "Oh Brody," she whispered, running her hand across his ripped abs, her fingers tracing down his hips and over to grip his tight ass muscles.

He reached down and lifted the hem of her jersey, throwing it to the other side of the room when she was free from it. For a moment, he just stood there, staring at her face then looking down at her near-naked body. "Jesus Christ, you're a living dream."

The charming words and the loving look in Brody's eyes clenched Taylor's heart like a fist. Hooking her fingers through his belt loops, she dragged him with her as she walked back until she felt the edge of her bed meet the back of her knees. She lay on the mattress, pulling his large form over her. His gaze traveled down her body, following the slow movement of his hand as he caressed her breasts, her ribs, her hips, and then her thighs. She shuddered as trails of goose bumps formed over the waves of heat caused by his touch. "How could I ever let a treasure like you escape me?" His voice was low and seductive, but it had a touch of sweet affection in it.

Taylor pulled his face so that he was looking right at her. "Brody?"

"What is it, baby?" He grazed her cheek with the back of his fingers.

She paused, relishing the passion and desire that swam in his brown, puppy dog eyes. "I love you, too."

* * * *

As Brody grazed Taylor's lush bottom lip with the pad of his thumb, he swallowed the tears threatening to leak from his eyes. Her soft, wet tongue slowly stroked his finger, ending with a quiet kiss.

There was still pain in her eyes, left to fester after Jay's evil words. She still longed for Jay, for he could sense it in the two tears falling on the pillow underneath her head. "Taylor, I know he hurt you, and he broke my heart, too—"

"Stop, Brody," she interrupted, her lip returning to a quivering state. "Please, I don't want to think about him right now. It's just me and you, and we're not scared to love each other, so that's all that matters."

As he lowered his head to kiss her, she began to slowly undo his belt buckle. He knew she was lying through her teeth when she said he was all that mattered. There was no doubt in his mind she was in love with him, but there was also no doubt she loved and needed Jay just as much. But he wouldn't think about that right now. Right now he would just make her feel better, show her how much he really loved her.

He'd tried to muffle his moan by burying his face in her neck when he felt the cool grip of her hand wrap around his warm shaft, but her smell only intensified his arousal. She didn't reek of heavy floral or dusty vanilla like the females he had bedded before. He smelled Taylor, the lightly scented lotion that made her skin heaven to touch, the talc powder scent that he had become addicted to.

She was taking way too long undressing him, so he stood up by the bed and completely undressed himself while he watched Taylor peel her boy shorts off, revealing the bare pussy he had yet to have the pleasure of pushing himself into. He eagerly looked her over, not able to decide just what ravishing part of her gorgeous body to settle his sight on.

He slowly climbed over her, resting his cock against her clit and lower stomach as they continued their erotic kissing. He heard her whimper softly as he began to grind against her pink clit, her moisture coating his length and sending her feminine scent straight to his head.

Supporting himself with his elbows, he cupped her breasts in his hands, amazed at the fullness of her flesh as he massaged them in a circular motion, her nipples beading beneath the grips of his thumbs and forefingers while he continued to gyrate against her clit.

When he looked up at her face, Taylor was staring at him, appearing to bite her lower lip in an effort to silence her reaction. The gold flecks in her eyes twinkled in the bright moonlight under lust-heavy eyelids.

"I can't believe I'm about to make love to the most beautiful creature I have ever seen, or could even imagine."

Taylor's eyes widened with surprise. He had to admit he was a little taken aback to see Taylor's shocked expression. If only she was able to see herself as others did, as he did, she would never suffer from any form of self-doubt.

He felt her body shudder beneath him as he lowered his head and buried his face in her large tits. Much to his delight, Taylor surrendered, begging him as he sucked on her nipples, covering them with his tongue. "Please," Taylor whispered. "I love you so much. I *need* you, Brody."

A growl came from his chest, his patience disappearing with the sound of his name being whispered as he pushed his cock through the lips of her pussy, her wet, hot flesh vacuuming him into a paradise of passion. He painfully bit his tongue very, very hard, hoping to quiet his moans while distracting himself from coming too soon.

* * * *

Taylor fisted the sheets at her sides as Brody impaled her quaking body with his enormous cock. "Ohh, ohh," she panted uncontrollably. She tried to gather the strength to restrain from being noisy, but despite her best efforts, the moans continued to form in the back of her throat.

"Shut up, baby," Brody urgently whispered. "You can't moan like that, or we'll get caught, okay?"

Taylor nodded apologetically then closed her eyes and tried to focus on remaining silent, struggling to ignore the pangs of sensations coursing through her limbs. But closing her eyes only made her aware of the soft, arousing slapping sounds of his balls spanking her ass cheeks with each forceful thrust. The loud smacking sounds caused another involuntary but inevitable moan to escape from her lips.

"Noisy little thing, aren't you?" He covered her mouth with his hand.

Taylor didn't expect the reaction her body had to being lightly gagged. She felt the cream in her pussy drip down to her rosebud at the realization of not being able to make the sounds her voice begged to create.

Brody slowly pumped in and out of her cunt, pushing at the hilt of her channel with each long stroke. Her heels dug into his lower back, and she raked her nails down his shoulders as his dick pumped pure electric ecstasy through her veins.

"Mmm, Taylor, I feel like I'm fucking silk." Another groan struggled to free itself through Brody's hand at the music of his whisper. Brody seemed to look around for something, then he finally grabbed the boy shorts that lay beside her. He stuffed the small cotton panties into her gaping, moaning mouth then again covered it with his hand to hold it in place as he continued to thrust inside her. Each thrust brought even stronger tingles to different parts of her heated body. Although she had only worn the panties for a short time after the shower she'd just taken, she could still taste a slight hint of her sweet, musky desire from when Brody was kissing her. The taste drove her wild with hunger for more kink.

Brody breathed heavy in her ear, vowing his love between his exerted pants. "You drive me crazy, Taylor. I could just die right now with my cock buried in this silky little pussy." Taylor bit down on the bundle of cotton stuffed between her jaws to keep from screaming out Brody's name.

Taylor breathed harder when Brody began to lightly lick and suckle on her sensitive ear lobe. "You're so beautiful, so perfect. Does it feel good, baby? Too bad you can't make a sound right now," he teased. The physical control he had over her turned her on beyond belief and had Taylor grinding her clit harder into his pelvis as he roughly plunged into her soaked cunt.

"Lift your arms above your head," he demanded. She immediately obeyed, loving this game way too much not to. With his left hand still firmly planted on her panty-stuffed mouth, Brody used his right hand to firmly hold down her wrists against the mattress while he continued to thrust his searing rod into her vulnerable body.

"Damn, girl, look at you." Brody exhaled through his pursed lips. "Look at these titties bounce as I pound this cock into your tight cunt. Look down, baby, and watch yourself." Taylor obeyed, straining to lift her head while she looked down to watch Brody's wide cock disappear and reappear from her body, its taut skin glistening with her musky juices.

The sight of his large frame fucking her senseless caused a thick gush of cream to trickle from her full opening. "Oomph! Fuck, baby." Yup, he definitely felt it drown his stiff cock. "You like watching me fuck you, don't you, princess? Your hot pussy juices are flooding around my dick."

Taylor could see Brody was wincing from the obvious strain of holding back. The vision threw sex gasoline on the wildfire that engulfed her insides. The panties in her mouth absorbed her primal moans, and the muffled sound seemed to pluck at Brody's arousal. Each thrust was so deep, so damn full, his great size creating a heavenly combination of blissful pleasure teetering on the edge of panicked pain. And after years of feeling the pressure to be Miss Perfect, it felt liberating to allow herself to become completely vulnerable to Brody's physical and emotional power over her.

Taylor felt her body tense with her on-coming orgasm when he reached down to pinch one of her swollen nipples, and her thighs began their signature violent shudder that only Jay and Brody could create. "Yeah, baby, come with me." As Taylor felt Brody's cock throb massively against her pussy walls, the sensation grabbed her entire being and celestial sparks burst from her core. Her muffled scream mixed with the heavy sounds of Brody's completion.

They lay still for a moment. Resting his forehead against hers, Brody's damp, warm body pressed against hers. "I love you," he whispered before freeing the panties from her mouth and rolling off of her. He pulled her close to his hot, naked body, and she snuggled her head in his muscular chest. She felt so feminine and adored as they lay there, Brody stroking her hair gently with his hand. The last thing she remembered was Brody pulling her hand to his lips for a gentle kiss while she was softly pulled into sleep.

Chapter 9

"I swear you're goin' to be late to your own funeral, Auntie."

"Child, you know I can't leave the house without having the perfect outfit," Veronica called out from upstairs. "What do you think?" she asked, grinning as she swayed down the steps. She was wearing a Michael Kors safari romper in a chic, dark khaki color, and she paired it with golden ribbon strap-up sandals and Chanel aviators.

Taylor smiled. "I think you look fabulous."

Aurora had called earlier that morning to check on Taylor, always endearingly sweet, and she had mentioned there was a fresh selection of the in-season produce at the local farmer's market. Veronica came up with a plan for a girls' day out for just the two of them while they made their way to the market to shop for dinner.

Over the last three days, Taylor had ignored all of Jay's attempts at apologizing, refusing to take his calls or come to the door when he came by looking for her. He was relentless with his attempts, but Taylor felt his cruel words were unforgivable.

Although Taylor's heart still ached, it was a beautiful day and she would be crazy not to take advantage. Besides, Aunt Veronica always made their girls' days exciting with her tales of multiple male suitors and old days at the Pink Floyd laser shows she would attend in Dallas.

Their first stop was going to be coffee and a fried egg with avocado sandwich on the patio at Breakfast at Stephanie's. Taylor's stomach growled in anger from being teased with a small glass of orange juice earlier that morning.

Taylor wore her favorite Diane Furstenberg piece. It was a dark aqua and lime printed ankle-length maxi dress with a plunging halter top that she had to wear without a bra. And since it draped so close to her curves, she couldn't wear panties, either, without her panty line showing. She wore her hair straight and natural, and her makeup consisted of a simple palette of blush, mascara, and lip stain.

"And you are just ravishing, sister," replied Aunt Veronica, cupping a cool hand against Taylor's cheek. Before Taylor could get out a thank you, there was a knock at the door. She and Veronica took a moment to exchange puzzled looks before Taylor turned to open it.

There on the front steps was a large Chanel shopping bag with a note attached. Taylor read it aloud as shock took over.

My Princess, I heard you and Ms. Veronica were having a day out, so I thought you could use a new day bag to carry your new stuff in. I hope you like it. I lost my head the other night, and although you may never forgive me, you still deserve the best I have to offer.

Love, Jay

This was all so confusing. Looking up at Aunt Veronica, Taylor said, "He's insane."

"Well, honey, don't you at least want to look at what's inside?"

"I don't care what's inside, Aunt Veronica. I told you what he said, and there's no way I could ever forgive him for that. I have Brody, and that's more than enough for me."

"Oh, Taylor, please!" Aunt Veronica slumped down on one of the bottom steps of the staircase as she shook her head as if she were growing impatient. "We both know there's a gaping hole in your heart that can only be filled by both Brody and Jay together. I've been living in this town long enough to know a woman bitten by the ménage bug when I see one. And once they're bit, honey, a single man will just no longer do."

Taylor had never been a good liar, and she couldn't bring herself to deny what Aunt Veronica was saying. "Well, if that's true, then we'll just find another man, a better man."

"Oh, Taylor," Aunt Veronica huffed as she crossed her arms. "You'll be able to find another, but we both know he won't be better, and he won't resuscitate you the way Jay did."

Taylor could only look down in response. Well, it wouldn't hurt to at least see what he bought her. As she lifted her gift out of the crisp tissue paper, her jaw dropped open. Aunt Veronica gasped loudly in amazement.

Taylor was holding in her very own hands the vintage-inspired Chanel diamond purse she had daydreamed of so many times before.

"Dear Lord, Taylor, that's almost a three-hundred thousand dollar purse!"

"I know," Taylor said after releasing a heavy sigh. Any woman not living under a rock knew all about the purse. It was the unicorn of fashion. Everyone had heard of it, but no one she knew ever had the pleasure of actually seeing it. There were only ten in the world, one of which belonged to Princess Camilla of Wales, and now one belonged to Taylor. It was a light-cream alligator skin with platinum buckle detailing and five carats worth of perfect diamonds in the shape of the designer's logo on the front flap. The purse was an absolutely breathtaking work of art.

"Well, don't just stand there, sister, put it on. You deserve it." Before Taylor could move, Aunt Veronica was pulling her old Coach purse off her arm. "Go on. Let me get a look at you with it."

Taylor's brain was still diamond-entranced, and she lethargically put the treasure on her shoulder and turned to the giant mirror by the couch. "Oh, Veronica, I can't accept this."

"Have you lost your mind?" Veronica cried as she came from behind her, her eyes bugging out in the reflection. "Jay knows he made a big mistake, and he bought you that to show you how sorry he truly is. No man is going to buy a purse for a woman that's worth more than most people's houses unless he is dead-serious about her."

Taylor couldn't believe Jay went to that extent just to say he was sorry. The more she stared at the reflection, the more the girl in her became attached to her royal gift. "Well, he did say some pretty nasty things, and this definitely qualifies as redemption."

* * * *

After their delectable brunch at Stephanie's, Taylor and Veronica walked across SoMale to the local bookshop. There was nothing like shelves of new hardbacks to lift Taylor's spirits. As usual, the women split up once they stepped into the shop. Veronica went to her home of erotic romance novellas, and Taylor headed to the classics.

Being a creature of habit when it came to her romance, Taylor scanned the endless rows of spines for Brontë. If she couldn't get lost in love in her own life, she always had Jane to live vicariously through. Right as she got to the B's, she saw something sitting neatly at the end of the shelf, right next to a beautiful, gold-spine edition of *Jane Eyre*. It was a large red envelope peeking from the books. Taking it in her hand, Taylor saw her name clearly written on the front of it. She tore it open and read the note, immediately recognizing Jay's unique handwriting from the earlier note.

To My Princess,
Anything you want in the store is yours. The employees have already been informed.
Love,
Jay

He remembered.
Taylor looked up from the letter to find the entire front desk of employees staring and smiling at her in reassurance, one young man even giving her a thumbs-up in excitement. She couldn't bite back the smile on her lips as she began to gather all the titles of her dreams.

* * * *

Taylor and Veronica left the store with a total of twelve full bags of books, magazines, CDs, box sets, and Blu-Ray discs. Taylor was still impressed with the fact Jay remembered the name of her favorite author and knew exactly where she would be looking in the store when he put the note in the bookshelf. She hadn't completely forgiven him yet, but she was starting to warm up to the idea.

As Taylor and Veronica walked into their favorite sushi bar for lunch, they were greeted by the staff like they were expecting them, giving them VIP treatment and everything on the house. Before they left, the waiter had brought over a fortune cookie for Veronica, but he handed Taylor a large jewelry box, giggled, and then walked off.

When Taylor opened it, she found a large fortune cookie made of white and pink diamonds and rose gold. She realized it was another purse when she saw the gold link chain strap and that it opened with a large diamond clasp. Inside was a long strip of satin with words on it.

"What does it say?" asked Veronica when Taylor burst out in laughter at the fortune she was given. Veronica eagerly grabbed the satin strip from Taylor's hand and read the fortune aloud. "'It is better to lose your pride with someone you love rather than to lose that someone you love with your useless pride.' I don't understand what's so funny."

"Oh come on, Veronica. Like I really believe Jay Stephens *loves* me."

When Aunt Veronica only lifted a brow with her obvious answer, Taylor cleared her throat and looked away in response to the awkward silence. There was an elephant in the room that Taylor just wasn't ready to acknowledge. Without further words, Taylor rose from her seat, gave a nod of thanks to the staff, and followed Aunt Veronica out the door.

They stopped by the farmer's market on the way home and picked up some produce for grilled peaches with blackberry-basil butter, which they planned to make later for dessert.

When they began the walk back to Aunt Veronica's house, twilight was just beginning to descend upon them. As they approached the porch steps, they found Jay sitting on the porch swing, looking as dashing and gorgeous, if not more so, as the day Taylor had met him, and he was holding a shoe box in his lap. He had on his gold aviator sunglasses, dark jeans, and another thin white button-down that was opened with a light under-tank peaking through. His leather watch matched his shoes. Taylor felt her nipples tighten at the mere sight of him. He looked like a white knight waiting for her return.

Aunt Veronica broke the heavy silence that hovered in the air. "I'll be inside if you need me, baby girl." She then disappeared into the house, closing the front door behind her.

"Hi," he said as he lifted his sunglasses from his face. The intense jade color had Taylor looking away bashfully. He still gave her that feeling, like she was an unworthy peasant girl being ogled by the unattainable Prince Charming. "I brought you something." He indicated the simple, light brown box he was holding.

"Let me guess, more diamonds?"

"Um, well." He paused as he searched for his words. "I mean, I wasn't exactly sure of what you would like, but every girl likes diamonds, right?"

Taylor couldn't argue with that, so she just raised her chin and looked down at the box, trying her best to hide her anticipation for her next gift. When she looked up at Jay, she realized he had been staring at her with dreamy eyes, lost in his own trance as he raked her face and body with his eyes.

"Oh yeah," he said when he realized he was staring, then he dropped to one knee as he placed the box on the ground.

When he looked up at her, he was holding out a Stuart Weitzman Cinderella slipper! She gasped at the surreal vision before her. The shoes were accessorized with hundreds of diamonds, and she knew from being in the pageant scene that they were worth well over two million dollars.

She grabbed it from his hand for a closer inspection. As she admired the beauty of the endless carats sparkling before her, she felt Jay feeling around her ankle.

"What are you doing?"

"I got you an anklet. You have the perfect feet for it." He was clasping a string of dark pearls and aqua gems around her ankle. It looked like it cost a fortune, and Taylor guessed it was from Stephanie's or somewhere close by. The aqua matched the dress she was wearing and was obviously intentional.

"Jay, what is all this? You've lost your mind."

"I accidently ruined your new Lubby Lu shoes, so it was only fair I replaced them."

"Louboutin," Taylor corrected with a giggle.

He smiled, seeming to be relieved that she laughed. "Yeah, that one." He rose to his feet and took her face in his hands, looking directly in her eyes. "Taylor, I can't live without your forgiveness. I can't live knowing you have no idea how I feel about you. I know you love Brody. He told me you've been seeing each other, and I want you to be happy, but I will never stop making the other night up to you. Never."

Jay walked back over to the porch swing and lifted something off the seat. He turned back to her and gave her a small bouquet of freshly picked wildflowers that had been wrapped in a paper towel. They were beautiful, and they looked oddly similar to the ones from Mrs. Abrams' beloved garden.

She tried to hold back the smile as she thought of her high-society Jay sneaking into old ladies' gardens to pick flowers for her. As much as she was smitten with the luxurious gifts of the day, the flowers had to have been the most amazing gift she had ever received.

* * * *

Jay waited for Taylor's reply as he watched her study her diamond sandal. *Please, God.*

"But you already know, don't you, Jay?" Taylor's eyes were misty when she looked up at him. "You knew that night in the car that I love you."

Jay scooped Taylor up in his arms and spun her on the porch, placing her back down on her feet to give her a hungry, needing kiss, the kiss he'd prayed to have again since that horrible night. She moaned softly as she returned his kiss just as passionately. The vibration of her intoxicating mouth sent hot currents of arousal straight to his growing cock. That's all it took for the sweet kiss to turn red hot.

Jay broke away from her mouth to look into her eyes. They were already gazing at him with lust, and Jay knew Taylor needed the same thing he needed.

* * * *

Taylor didn't protest when Jay grabbed her hand and led her to the back of Aunt Veronica's house. Once they rounded the corner, Taylor shrieked in surprise as Jay suddenly shoved her frame against the wall, his body pressed firmly against hers.

Before she had a chance to question his dominating behavior, Jay immediately dove in to give her a wildly passionate kiss, his swirling, talented tongue distracting her from talking. She felt both his hands grasp the thin straps of her maxi dress then he yanked the material down to rest on her hips, leaving her breasts hanging naked in the moist Texas air.

A low, lustful growl came from Jay, his eyes transfixed on her swollen tits. The way his eyes danced in passion from just looking at her made Taylor feel beautiful, sexy, and womanly. She leaned forward to touch him, but Jay placed a large palm on her breast bone and shoved her against the back of the house. "Put your arms around my neck," he commanded as he looked deep in her eyes.

Taylor let out a soft laugh. "But the neighbors—"

"They can watch."

Taylor felt her eyes widen at his indifference to their surroundings.

"Arms, Taylor. Now." Taylor silently obeyed, the domination in his tone making her exposed clit throb against the material of her dress.

Jay reached down and quickly undid his belt and jeans before pushing them down his thighs. Then he used his impressive strength to lift her ass with his free hand, and her legs were wrapped around his waist, her wet pussy perfectly lined with his jutting, steel-hard cock.

"Fuck, baby. Someone's a bad girl," Jay whispered against her ear as he leaned forward and the head of his cock discovered she wasn't wearing any panties. One of his hands tugged at her nipples as he took her in another heated, longing kiss as his throbbing dick sought entrance.

Taylor let out a loud, surprised gasp when Jay pounded his enormous length deep into her creaming cunt.

"Mmm, my God, Taylor. You're already about to come, aren't you, baby? I can feel your pussy milking my cock. It's hungry for more, isn't it, baby?"

Taylor was embarrassed at her body's eager reaction, but she nodded anyway. "Yes, Jay. Make me come. Please, please."

Jay groaned and leaned down to take a breast in his mouth as he pounded her hard against the house. Taylor immediately felt her body tighten in anticipation of her intense climax, and suddenly it felt like every part of her, pussy, tits, limbs, heart, was on fire.

"Yeah, Taylor. Let me hear you come, baby. Let me hear you cry out my name." Jay pounded harder, and he moaned as he spilled his hot cum inside her. His cock pulsed violently, and the strong force had Taylor's orgasm spilling over her like molten lava.

"So good, oh my God. Jay!" She felt her body jerk as the tortuous waves of desire washed over her. She could still feel his cock throbbing inside her as she slowly came back to earth.

Jay gently placed her back on the ground before kissing her again. His breaths were was still short, and his skin glistened with the exertion of their lovemaking.

"I'm so sorry, baby," he whispered against her warm lips. "You're the one I want, and it scared the living shit out of me. But I have one more surprise for you." He pulled the spaghetti straps of her dress back up over her shoulders, redressing her gently.

Taylor let out a soft giggle. "Let me guess."

"Actually, I'm out of gifts right now, but I think you'll still like it."

"Look, about these gifts—"

"Don't insult me, Taylor," he interrupted. "You're a princess, I told you that. And as long as you're with me and Brody, you'll need to get used to living the lifestyle of one. We refuse to have it any other way."

Just then, Brody came from the side of the house.

When Taylor saw him, she cried out, "Brody!" as if she hadn't seen him in years. She wrapped her arms around his neck and kissed him as he lifted her from the ground and set her in front of him.

"We promise you won't regret this, Taylor. We're going to make you the happiest woman on Earth, you'll see." The love in Brody's eyes as he looked at her was dark and intense. He turned to Jay. "You know, Taylor is technically a beauty *queen*, not a princess."

Taylor pouted. "Oh, Brody, can't I just remain a princess? They're so much younger than queens." She turned and winked at Jay playfully, and the men laughed, shaking their heads.

"Even in their twenties, southern belles are so damn sensitive about their age." Jay chuckled.

"Wait a minute, were you there the whole time, Brody?"

Brody wiggled his eyebrows playfully and gave her ass a hard smack but didn't answer her question.

"Yeah," Jay stepped forward, "and about that surprise."

Chapter 10

When he interrupted their playtime for Taylor's next surprise, Jay noticed the disappointed look on her face, but she had complied. He parked the truck in his huge driveway, relieved his parents' car was nowhere in sight. For Mom and Pops, Wednesdays were reserved for bingo followed by an evening picnic at the lake.

Jay got out of the car in eager anticipation, and Brody held Taylor's hand as they followed Jay to the backyard. The sun was now reduced to an orangey hot pink strip on the graying horizon.

He hadn't been in his parents' secret garden in years, and never intended on going back, but as he moved closer to its walls, he was more than eager to break through his fear. For some reason, all he wanted was to see Taylor's reaction to the mystical world his fathers had built. It was a baffling itch he had to scratch right then.

"Oh, my God. This is amazing." Taylor gasped as they made their way deeper into the massive land of cobblestone paths, perfectly trimmed bushes of every size, and hundreds of beds of exotic flowers. The dim outdoor lamps were already putting spotlights on random parts of the estate.

"Oh, actually, we haven't come to the best part yet," Jay said, smiling when Taylor's eyes widened in excitement.

He turned and spotted the four, twenty-foot stone walls that were covered in lush, green moss, and he felt a sudden sick feeling in his gut. He stopped in his path and turned to look over his shoulder. Brody was holding aside a curtain of vines as Taylor cautiously made her way toward Jay, and then she looked up and gave him that signature innocent, virginal smile, her deep, angelic dimples perfectly centered on her rosy cheeks. Jay turned back around and closed his eyes for a couple of seconds as he breathed deeply in then out, trying to push down the nervous ball building in his chest.

"Wow!" Taylor strained her neck to look up at the tall walls. "What is this place?"

Brody only gave her a smile, and Jay began to search the area for the key to the door. He then remembered his mother always hid it under the baby cupid statue in the middle of the birdbath that sat at his left. His stomach dropped with anxiety when he felt the familiar, cool steel of the antique key. He took a moment to study it, running his fingers along the fancy swirl pattern. It had been so long since he held it, and he was a little surprised it looked exactly as he remembered. His mother's proud, ecstatic voice echoed in his head. *And the key is just as perfectly divine as the garden.*

"Jay? Did you find the key?" Brody's voice brought Jay back.

Jay made his way over to the door and inserted the key into the rusty hole. The door creaked loudly as he slowly pushed it open, revealing a whole other world to the trio. Jay braced himself for another sick feeling in his stomach, but a surprising feeling of contentment poured over him as he watched Taylor run toward the garden swing, squealing in delight as she jumped up on the high seat.

Brody stepped closer to Jay's side, and they both watched in silence as Taylor hung her head back, her eyes closed as she held onto the ropes on either side of her, swinging back and forth in a smooth motion. The summer Texas humidity left a dewy glaze on her pretty, delicate face, and her hair was beginning to form natural waves in the damp climate. The heat of the day had made the deep v-neck of Taylor's dress limp with the moisture of the air, revealing more cleavage than it was probably intended to show.

Jay just noticed she must have kicked off her heels when he saw her feet with their cherry red toenails sway gracefully under the swing bench. The new anklet he bought her made her feet look even more delicate. She looked so peaceful and so happy, Jay's heart jumped with a sudden jolt of emotion, but he managed to swallow it down to speak.

"You know, that's the first thing Mama did, too, when Papa Craig and Papa Clark showed her the garden."

Brody turned to give him a soothing, closed-lip smile, squeezing the back of Jay's neck in a masculine show of affection, then walked over to Taylor.

* * * *

If this is a dream, I never want to wake up.

She hovered several feet above the ground, enough to feel as though she were flying when she closed her eyes. She relished the warm twilight breeze that whispered across her face and body, not wanting to open her eyes in fear it would all disappear.

When she heard a twig snap beneath heavy footsteps, she instinctively opened her eyes to see her men walking toward her. She smiled when she realized they must have been watching her for a couple of minutes by now.

"What do you think?" Jay indicated the paradise around them.

"It's perfection," Taylor purred, letting her head fall back again as she swung through the air.

And it was perfection. When Jay opened the garden door, a completely different universe was exposed to her eyes. They were surrounded by a rainbow of wild flowers, small, round bushes, tall bushes that were trimmed to resemble bunny rabbits and birds with spread wings, dozens upon dozens of potted plants that looked like they all came from different parts of the world, and blankets of moss and vines that spread up the stone walls. In the back right corner was a Balinese canopy daybed made of cherry wood and surrounded by snow white linen curtains. It was the biggest daybed she had ever seen, at least twice as big as a king. She imagined falling asleep on its dozens of Mediterranean pillows in the summer rays, drifting off to the Lone Star song of the mockingbirds. *Maybe I died in a car accident on the way here, and now I'm in heaven.*

Taylor realized she was thinking aloud when she heard the men laugh. She dropped her gaze down in time to see both Jay and Brody peel off their designer shirts. Taylor swallowed hard as her eyes raked over every chiseled muscle of their torsos. Their shoulders looked even broader when they weren't hidden under clothes, and her eyes traveled down over their well-formed six-packs to their enticing muscular thighs.

"Well," Jay said as he began to work the square silver buckle on his leather belt, "if that pretty flush in your cheeks is any indication, you're still very much alive."

She watched in anticipation as the men undressed, revealing more off their golden, glistening skin. She looked down at the enormously thick, long erections that pointed up at her, taunting her with pulsing veins and drops of pre-cum. She had been haunted by images of their hard-ons since the day at the lake, and she licked her lips at the thought of finally taking them both into her body at once.

They walked toward her like moths to a flame, their eyes glued to the bright cotton material of the long summer dress that clung to her tits and hips. They looked like children in awe of a Christmas tree, and she smiled at their raw reaction to her, despite her being fully dressed.

She slowed down her swinging to a complete stop, and Jay dropped on one knee, then the other, his eyes boring into hers as he ran a rough hand under her dress to the top of her thigh, sending a shock of heat to her core. Brody then approached and fully lifted the hem of her dress so it rested on her thighs, then he caressed her left knee with his fingertips, slowly moving up her leg and sending a shiver of pleasure from his touch to her throbbing pussy. She gasped at the intense need for a more satisfying caress. Brody smiled, his eyes flickering in a lustful fire as he, too, dropped to his knees in front of her.

She watched both men lower their heads at the same time to give her a kiss on the tender spot just above her knees. The visual of two different men, a head of short, dark hair on her right and a head of dark-blond, messy waves on her left, caused her to release an unintentionally desperate whimper.

She grasped the swing ropes tightly when she saw their tongues dart out, tasting her dewy skin with their warm lips. The contact of her naked skin with their hot tongues caused Taylor to flinch at the unexpected jolt of intense sensation it created, and she could feel her opening already pulsating as it begged for the intimidating, beautiful, long cocks that stood at attention from their naked, tanned bodies.

Jay straightened, his emerald eyes now a dark forest green as he looked at Taylor to give her a sexy wink, then his eyes dropped to her body as he fisted the neckline of her dress in both hands and tore it straight down the middle.

"My dress!" she protested immediately. "That's the second one you've ruined, Jay."

He kneeled back down and grabbed her tits roughly with his large hands, the pleasure-pain making her gasp. "I'll buy you the whole damn store, baby. Now shut up and take it like a good girl." He took a pebbled nipple into his lips in a soft tug, causing her to lose control of her aching cunt, now grinding the swing bench in desperation.

The humid breeze felt like Heaven against her naked body as it mixed with the French kisses that were now making their way up her inner thighs. Taylor arched her body as she leaned back into the breeze, her hands still holding on to the swing ropes and her eyelids dropping as she relished the most amazing moment of her life. *In this moment, everything is perfect, everything is beautiful, everything is a dream.*

When she felt the delectable warmth radiate from their mouths as they inched closer to her creaming cunt, she opened her eyes to witness the moment she was dying for since she spotted her fine-ass men driving their cousins' four-wheelers in front of her house. Brody placed a hand on Taylor's lower back to support her balance as Jay spread her knees farther apart. The moist night breeze tickled her exposed folds, cooling the heat at her opening.

"Ooh." Jay let out a deep, heavy breath at the sight of her freshly waxed mound then leaned down to drag the firm, stiff tip of his tongue up through her slit, and ending with a lightning-quick suck on her clit. "Mmm, I'm never going to get over how good you taste, Taylor."

The last thing Taylor expected when Jay put his head between her thighs was for him to lick her in such a taboo place, shrieking louder when she suddenly felt Brody's tongue lavishing her left nipple.

Brody stood and gently pulled her face toward his as he took her in the most passionate, needy kiss she had ever experienced. He held tightly to the back of her head, moaning loudly and eagerly against her mouth. He tasted so sweet, and she groaned at the arousing mint flavor of his mouth. Everything about them was perfect.

She heard Jay hiss loudly as he pushed two fingers inside her until his knuckles pressed against the opening of her channel. Again, her pussy welcomed him without effort as he glided through its natural, abundant lubricant, and Jay stopped to stare at her face, watching as she lost control in her arousal.

"Holy shit!" she screamed when she released Brody's kiss with her sudden reaction. She attempted to reach down to press Jay's fingers deeper into her, but she quickly grabbed the rope back when she realized letting go would cause her to fall back and on the ground.

Brody covered both of her hands with his as they wrapped around the ropes. He leaned in to give a gentle lick to the side of her neck and whispered in her ear, "These stay here. If you let go, you'll just lose your balance." The thought of not being able to use her hands only made Taylor writhe more violently with impatience, but she followed his sultry command. The thought of her hands being confined was incredibly frustrating, yet incredibly erotic.

Brody returned to give her mouth another primal tongue-fucking. She wasn't sure if it was intentional or not, but he began to suck on her tongue in coordination with Jay's fingers as he dipped in the juices of her pussy. Brody tugged her right nipple in a circular-motion, firm but still too gentle for Taylor to grasp the sparkling ball of sensations that hovered just above her reach.

She continued to cry out in pleasure as she rocked her hips to their rhythm, and Brody responded by pinching her nipple harder. "Ohh, *yeah.*" Taylor squealed at Brody's touch, and Jay groaned as he dug his fingers deeper, moving them in a come-here motion and hitting a sweet spot Taylor never knew existed.

The intensity of the pleasure seemed too much for Taylor to handle, and she begun to wiggle her body to escape Jay's fingers. "Wait. It's too much..." But he just squeezed her right hip tightly with his other hand to keep his fingers inside. She had absolutely no strength in her to fight against his strong grip. He swung the swing in a short motion that allowed Taylor to buck her hips in a smooth, graceful rhythm with his hands. She panted and moaned, imagining ripples of electrical currents cascading her vulnerable body like gigantic waves.

The hottest idea came to her when she turned to watch Brody flick his flexed tongue over her nipple, and then watched as he relaxed it into a soft, wide muscle, swiping slowly over her full breast. "Brody?" Her voice came out in a husky whisper, and Brody looked up. "I want you to taste my pussy while Jay fingers me."

A shocked look appeared on Brody's face, and he looked down at a smiling Jay then back at Taylor. His eyes dropped to watch her heaving chest as she breathed heavily, then he looked up to shoot her a sultry, devilish smile.

She watched as Brody knelt down beside her and moved his mouth in to taste her. But instead of licking her like she expected, he cocked his head to the side, and he gently held her swollen clit between his smooth teeth with the perfect amount of pressure, his hazy eyes looking up to meet hers as if he were measuring her reaction. Taylor grasped the ropes of the swing tighter and screamed out as she felt his teeth nibble in coordination with the strong pulses of her engorged clit, soft then hard, soft then hard.

And God help her, she about melted out of the seat of the swing when she then felt the deliciously warm tip of his tongue barely brush back and forth over the captured nub while he continued to lightly squeeze it in his teeth.

"Please, please take me." The desperation in Taylor's voice may have been obvious, but all she was concerned about was grabbing a hold of the gratification she was chasing. Her embarrassment would have to wait.

Both men smiled up at her words. Jay continued the steady, short rock of the swing, still holding her in place by the hip, his fingers now digging deeper in her skin as she saw his face flush with arousal from watching her.

She immediately felt the torpedo of her on-coming orgasm whirl violently within her as she watched Brody's mouth work her pussy on the outside while Jay used his fingers to work her inside. "I'm—I'm coming," she struggled to announce as her building climax began to steal her breath. Brody groaned at her statement, changing from nibbles to strong, long sucks on the swollen, pink bud, and Jay lifted up to suck on the nipple closest to him. Her body shook, and she cried out as the waves of lust morphed into tsunamis of passion.

Both men held her firmly in place, their touches softening as she descended back to reality. But before she could catch her breath, Jay lifted her, and her legs wrapped around his torso, her still sensitive clit riding against his hard length as he carried her to the daybed. The large, weatherproof mattress was softer than she expected.

* * * *

Brody kept his eyes on those feminine, cherry red toenails as he followed Jay and Taylor to the bed in the corner of the garden's stone walls. Taylor's legs were a shimmering gold with the mix of her aroused sweat and the sticky humidity of the Texas night. The sight of them wrapped around Jay's muscular body had Brody stroking his near-painful erection before he even realized what he was doing.

He watched as Jay gently placed their pin-up on the huge mattress, her legs still dangling over the edge. Jay got to his knees and began making a trail of licks and soft kisses down her shins to her delicate, perfectly pedicured feet.

Taylor propped up on her elbows to keep eye contact with Jay. Taking her new anklet in his teeth, Jay looked up and winked at her. When he grabbed her small foot and began to flick her big toe with his tongue, Taylor bit her lower lip as she smiled, her eyes slowly closing before she moaned his name.

Jay stood, the movement causing his engorged cock and balls to bounce. He then took Taylor's little feet in his hands and guided the arches over his dick. Jay hissed loudly as he increased the speed of the friction along his length.

All Brody could think about was plunging his cock deep inside her dripping pussy. He walked over to the bed, and Taylor gave him a knowing, mischievous grin. The erotic look across her angelic face made Brody's cock twitch in response.

"Come here, Brody," she told him through her rosy, heart-shaped lips as she reached out to him. He still couldn't believe how gorgeous she was. As flawless as her doll face was, her body was lethal, perfectly formed in every way, lush curves below and above a tiny waistline.

Brody grabbed her hand, and Taylor pulled him over her as she reclined back. Jay continued to lick and massage her feet as Brody straddled her body. They kissed softly and slowly, a deep contradiction to her wet cunt gyrating in a ferocious hunger against his sensitized balls, his hard, pulsing length pressed between their damp bodies.

Jay moved to the bed, watching them as he pulled at his dick. "Ride Brody for me, baby. *Now!*" Jay's commanding voice seemed to bring out the primal tigress in Taylor as she immediately pushed Brody down on his back, straddling him in a shocking quickness. She clasped her lips down on his right nipple, tasting him with her smooth tongue, sending chills of need straight to his drooling cock. "*Shit*, Taylor. Ohh!" Brody licked his lips at the sensation of her tiny form taking over his large body as he raked his fingers through her silky strands.

He slowly pushed his body farther up on the bed, and Taylor followed his lead, crawling on the bed as she began a steaming trail down his body with her tongue. When he settled, his entire body was splayed on the mattress, and Taylor hovered over him on all fours, making her way down to his jumping cock. She grabbed his shaft firmly and immediately gave it a long, wet lick as she kept her eyes on his.

"Oh, Brody," she whispered between the bewitching sucks of her amazingly talented mouth, "I want you both inside me so bad," another tantalizing suck followed by the echo of his own husky groan, "I've been waiting much," another long lick, "much too long."

No longer able to control himself, Brody grabbed Taylor's shoulders firmly and pulled her over him. A shocked gasp escaped her mouth when he pushed her down on his length, and he felt his cock enter her warm, snug sheath with her silky cream offering little resistance.

* * * *

The sight of Brody's cock disappearing into Taylor's writhing little body and the sound of two sexual moans echoing against the garden's stone walls, had Jay squeezing the base of his cock in an effort to control his on-edge arousal. He slowly moved behind Taylor, his knees straddling Brody's shins as he watched his best friend grab her ass and fiercely bounce her high in the air, allowing his glistening cock to penetrate her deeply, over and over. Her sobs of arousal got louder the harder he bounced her.

"Slow down, Brody," Jay commanded, his voice low and insistent. When his friend didn't stop right away, Jay raised his voice. "*Brody.*"

Obediently, Brody let out a deep breath as he slowed down, his eyes closed and his face contorted, likely from the strain of holding back.

Taylor turned her head to join Jay in a passionate kiss while he scooped some thick cream from her opened cunt that still housed Brody's dick. He stroked his oiled fingers up to her tight asshole, preparing her for his large cock. He slowly pushed a finger through the tight ring of muscle, and he felt Taylor clench at the foreign intrusion.

"Relax, sugar. It'll only hurt a moment, I promise" he whispered in her ear. She only gave him a nod in answer and closed her eyes as she waited.

Jay withdrew his finger and knelt down to replace it with his watering tongue. With a hand on each ass cheek, he squeezed them together, allowing them to hug the sides of his face as he feasted on her asshole and dripping pussy. He groaned at the spicy-sweet taste as he tried his best to keep Taylor's writhing body as still as he could. The more she moaned and pushed back on his face, the shorter his fuse was getting. "I need my cock to stretch this beautiful ass right now, baby." He straightened and led his purple-tinged dick to her now-wet ass. He growled deeply as he entered her virgin ass.

"Ow! Jay, slow down," Taylor begged.

"Sorry, baby," he replied as he stroked her spine in reassurance. He slowly withdrew the tip and pushed it gently back in, repeating the motion until he slowly inched his entire length into her ass. He felt

Taylor relax after a few moments, and her breathless gasps soon became moans of pleasure.

"Oh, fuck, she's so damn tight," Brody exclaimed under Taylor. His breathing grew heavy and loud, the sound bringing Jay's passion out of control. Jay grabbed her fleshy hips, ready for the ride of his life as the men found a rhythm of lifting and pushing their wanton, shrieking woman down and over their lengths, each man taking turns to plunge their throbbing dicks deep in Taylor's welcoming body.

* * * *

The pleasure that followed the brief, sharp pain of Jay's intrusion was incredible. Taylor guessed double penetration with two average-sized cocks would be overwhelming in itself, but she had two enormously gifted men filling her body beyond its natural capacity.

Taylor struggled to find a focus as electric currents of pleasure pumped from both her fucked ass and pussy. A third current came to life when Brody licked his fingers and began tweaking both her nipples in succession with their thrusts.

She forced her eyes open as she watched more beads of sweat form across Brody's divine body. She noticed how tightly Jay's fingers squeezed her hips, and she knew he was enjoying himself as much as she was. Turning back to him, their eyes locked in a lustful trance.

"Spank me," she commanded in a husky voice.

"What?" Jay panted between strokes.

"I've been a bad girl, Mr. Stephens. Don't you wanna punish me?"

* * * *

A loud smack echoed through the garden as Jay's hand landed against Taylor's bouncing ass. Hearing his name spoken so formally against such a raunchy scene made Jay drop the tight grasp he barely had over his sexual control. *Smack!* The sounds echoed within the garden walls and seemed to make all three of them moan louder.

"Oh yeah, punish that naughty ass," Brody encouraged.

Smack!

Once he heard his and Brody's names being screamed, every muscle in Jay's body contracted and his eyes rolled back. He grunted loud breaths as he pumped to completion deep inside Taylor's wiggling ass.

At the exact moment his taut balls began to empty, he felt Taylor's thighs quiver against him, the mark of her oncoming orgasm making him smile. Her scream rose in volume, followed by a drawn out curse from Brody. Her body froze then shook, and she landed against Brody's chest.

As Jay looked down at the two bodies, all connected as one, he thought how heavenly they all looked out in the garden, and he thought about how much he loved the exhausted angel before him. The three of them were a perfect fit, as if their bodies were meant for each other.

I wonder what time Stephanie's opens tomorrow...

Chapter 11

"Motherfucker!"

Amber flinched at the burning contact made between her swollen crotch and the ice-pack she just prepared. She carefully settled back down on her pink-gingham-covered canopy bed, making sure the ice-pack was resting ever so gently on her naked, inflamed flesh as she sat cross-legged in front of her laptop.

Her teacup poodle, Cinderella, lay at the head of the bed, her chronic nervousness shaking her tiny, pink-dyed body like a leaf in her Juicy Couture, black doggie sweatsuit. She should've learned long ago to stay far from Amber when she was in one of her moods, or she'd likely find a shoe up her ass. Again…

The boy lying next to Amber was snoring so fucking loud she slapped the back of his head with the palm of her hand. "I can't fucking think straight when you're so damn loud, you damn pansy!" Amber promised herself it would be the last time she would take home a barback. They were always so damn young and so damn annoying. This one couldn't have been more than nineteen.

The boy barely moved an inch, only continuing to lie in a deep, drunken state. She couldn't remember his name, but she wasn't really trying to either. Just another jackhammer-thrusting, eager, faceless kid that looked better after eight Tito vodka sours than he did right now.

Turning her attention back to the computer, she typed in the address for the Web site that had been ruining her life for the past few days. Just when she thought it couldn't get any worse…

Amber Fox or Amber Fux? 23 Men Come Forward, Claiming Fox Had Sex for Coke and Diet Pills!

Amber threw her laptop against the wall with all her strength, and shattered pink and black pieces fell to the ground.

The young boy ran out the door with a blanket barely wrapped around his lower half as the most ear-piercing, screeching, glass-shattering scream came from Amber's mouth, and she didn't stop until she was completely out of breath.

Cinderella ran under the bed to take cover, her Coach doggie stilettos tripping her up, her legs scattering in a panic. Then Amber stood there, her chest heaving up and down as she struggled to return her breathing back to normal. All she could hear was Cinderella's fearful whimpers at her feet.

"This is all because of that spoiled little *bitch*, Taylor!" Amber could tell she was losing her mind, but she really, really didn't give a shit. "I *made* her! She was nothing but common trailer park trash until she met me, and now she thinks she can just ruin my life with her Noxzema face and last season's Prada shoes! We'll see about that!"

Sure, Taylor might not have directly destroyed Amber's chances at Miss Dallas Texas Yellow Rose, but Amber felt that if Taylor would have just allowed her to compete in the pageant alone and stop ruining her dreams by stealing every title Amber had wanted since they were thirteen, she wouldn't have had to run her out of town by having a ménage a trois with Dillon.

Suddenly, a light bulb went off in Amber's head. Grabbing her cell phone from her bedside table, she quickly scrolled down her contacts to Emilio Estefan.

The phone rang twice before he answered. "Why hello, *mija*! I was waiting for your call. Care to comment on my fabulous, new article?"

"Fuck off, Emilio. I'm not calling about your trashy articles."

"Now, Ambueler—"

"It's *Amber*, Emilio! Stop the wisecrack bullshit!"

Emilio let out a hearty laugh. "*Con permiso*, Senorita Amber. Please, what can I do for you?"

"First of all, I don't give a fuck about those washed-up, pencil-dick douche bags coming forward. My life was already ruined once you posted those pictures outside of Plush. Nothing could be worse than not being Miss Dallas Texas Yellow Rose." Amber paused to wipe the tear that ran down her cheek, took a dramatic breath to calm down, and then continued. "Now, what I called about is a little more… *sensational* than the petty dirt you have on me."

There was a long pause on the other end, then finally Emilio said, "I'm listening, senorita."

"Well, Daddy told me Taylor ran off to stay with her aunt and is supposedly dating Brody Bartlett. A friend of Daddy's saw him slipping into her window last night, as a matter of skanky fact."

Emilio gasped on the other end of the line. "Brody Bartlett? As in—"

"Yes, *the* Brody Bartlett. I swear, Little Miss Perfect thinks she's so damn untouchable. Well, what if I told you I might be able to get a little sex tape featuring our little Barbie and Ken?"

"*Pff!* Of Taylor Ewing? How the hell do you plan to pull that off?"

"Are you kidding? Don't let that virginal face fool you, Emilio. Dillon told me Taylor is quite the hellcat in bed, and I'm willing to bet she's got Brody with his pants around his ankles every minute of the day. All you need to do is find out where she is, and I'll find a way to catch them in the act." Amber remembered the "creeper box," as she called it as a child, that her father kept under his bed. Along with the "golden shower" porn, double-sided dildos, and anal beads, her father kept a small collection of state-of-the-art micro camcorders.

"I thought you said your *Papi* has all the latest news?"

"I tried to get him to tell me where she is, but he just mumbled something like telling me would be a liability, or some bullshit."

Emilio let out a robust laugh louder than the first irritating one. "*Aye ya yi*, even *Papi* Fox knows he planted a bad seed."

"Go to hell, Emilio. At least my father didn't abandon me for being a queer!"

"Yes, the very least," Emilio managed to say between uncontrollable giggles.

"Look, do you want the deal or not? I'll bring the sex tape if you post it. Deal?"

"Are you kidding? Dallas's very own Princess Diana caught doing the nasty with Texas billionaire playboy Brody Bartlett? It has *Cochina* of the Week written all over it! Give me two minutes to send my secret sources out, and I'll get right back to you." Emilio was infamous for never divulging the identity of his anonymous sources.

Exactly two minutes after Amber hung up, her phone rang. "She's just an hour east of here on the interstate. It's a little town called Male Order."

Chapter 12

Taylor felt like a princess that had been rescued from a life as a peasant, only there were two princes instead of one. Jay crawled into the back of the limo then turned and reached for her hand to help her in. Brody held her waist from behind with both hands, like she was a glass sculpture to protect. None of the snot-nosed little boys of her past had ever made her feel this way.

"Let me guess, another surprise?" Taylor was sitting between her men when the limo driver closed their door, a gust of the warm night air blowing her bangs across her eyes.

"Of course," the men casually replied in unison.

Already used to her involuntary response, Taylor squeezed her thighs together when she felt her moisture make its way from her pulsating entrance. She couldn't help but feel a little guilty for soiling her new Dolce dress (well, her *only* Dolce dress). It was the perfect little black number, sexy yet simple enough to let her sequin Louboutins take center stage.

Brody brushed his lips on her bare shoulder from her right, instantly putting her body in a relaxed state with his soft, sweet humming. Right as she rolled her head back, she felt Jay's lips press against hers.

"Mmm," Taylor softly moaned as she kissed her alpha prince back. Usually, by now, Jay would have her mouth in an erotic dance with his tongue, but surprisingly, he kept his kiss soft. She moaned again in hopes it would encourage him to be more aggressive, but he still held back, keeping the kiss sweet and romantic.

Taylor grabbed the back of Jay's neck and pulled him closer as she opened her lips in invitation.

"Baby, wait," said Jay as he pulled back a little.

"Why? What's wrong?" Taylor felt in her gut that something strange was up. She felt it in his touch and saw it in how weird he had been acting since they had picked her up from Aunt Veronica's. She swallowed at the thought of him not wanting her anymore. She had been waiting for Jay to tell her he loved her, and she had thought two nights ago on the porch would be that moment. But he never even mentioned the subject.

"If you keep that up, you're going to ruin the surprise," Brody answered for him when Jay hesitated to reply, then continued to sprinkle her shoulder and arm with kisses.

When she saw the lust swimming through Jay's eyes, she realized he really was holding back but not from not wanting her, so it had to be a good reason. She smiled in anticipation of what the surprise might be.

When she looked out the window, she could see they were driving farther into the country night, but she couldn't see anything else. Suddenly, about three dozen brightly-colored hot air balloons came into view, and her heart dropped.

"Oh God," she whispered, in fear. She looked down at her lap and saw she was fisting her new dress, so she quickly let go. Her hands had already left damp spots on the expensive material.

"Jesus, Taylor, are you okay?" Brody pulled her face to his. "You're as white as a ghost, princess."

"I—I can't go up." Taylor could already feel the dizzying panic start to kick in, and they hadn't even parked yet. Taylor's biggest phobia was heights. She wasn't even able to go up an escalator without getting vertigo.

"Taylor, look at me." Jay's voice was demanding and dominating but not angry. When she did, he said, "You have nothing to worry about. We would never, ever let anything happen to you, I forever promise you that." For a second, that word, forever, warmed Taylor's sunken heart, and she forgot about the rainbow balls of death in the background for a moment.

But when Jay suddenly turned away at the sound of the chauffeur opening his door, her trance was broken, and she was once again scared to death.

"Can you feel it?" Brody whispered tenderly in Taylor's ear. "Can't you feel we would never do anything to hurt you?" She nodded, and she felt his grip on her shoulder tighten a bit when he kissed the top of her head as it rested on his chest. "I swear to you, Taylor, as long as you're with us, you will never feel pain."

Taylor's body immediately stopped trembling. Brody's words eased her aching heart and soothed her terror. She looked up at him, then turned to Jay, and saw the same honesty she always saw in their eyes. She realized then that the love between her and Brody and Jay could last forever because not only did they have the passion, they had the trust. It was the first time in Taylor's life she felt that with any man. And then there were two.

She kissed Brody softly, relishing the clean smell of his skin and the intoxicating wetness of his mouth. He lovingly brushed the back of his hand across her cheek as they kissed, and he gave a soft moan against her lips. He tasted so sweet, and he touched her like she was a precious gem.

* * * *

When Jay turned back to them, Brody was holding the tiny, trembling goddess against his chest, gently brushing his fingers through her auburn hair as he whispered encouraging, sweet words in her ear. He could see it was slightly relaxing her as she nodded at Brody's words. He watched as Taylor lifted her head and gave Brody a romantically soft kiss in appreciation as a tear of fear slowly trickled down her cheek.

It was definitely time to jump off the edge.

"Come on, princess." Jay reached out a hand, leading Taylor onto the open field. Her small palm grew warm and clammy as it squeezed his tightly with tension. Wrapping an arm around her shoulders, he held her against him as they walked toward the largest among the balloons.

Jay could feel that Brody's words had relaxed her a little, but fear still radiated from her body. They met an older gentleman at the basket. He wore his long, silver hair in braided pigtails and had a red bandana wrapped around his forehead.

"Alrighty, you three. This here is the hot air balloon you reserved, and this here is the rope that'll be connected to y'all and the ground. No horseplay, no loogies, no littering, no shaking the basket…" The old man rambled the safety instructions, obviously bored from years of the same script.

Jay looked down and saw Taylor had her eyes closed, her thick, dark eyelashes fanned out against her pink cheeks, and she was breathing deeply through her nose then slowly releasing it through her shiny lips. Yet, she hadn't uttered a single protest since she'd stepped out of the limo. He couldn't help but smile at her bravery. Anyone looking at Taylor could see she was as feminine as a powder puff, but anyone lucky enough to actually know her knew she was as determined as a bull.

* * * *

"You payin' attention there, girl?" The old man's scornful voice forced Taylor's eyes open.

"Yes, sir," she mumbled as she looked up at the monstrosity in front of her.

"It's Miss Ewing, *sir*." She heard Jay correct the old grump in defense, but she tried her best to focus on the colors of the hot air balloon as both men pulled her toward the basket.

Yellow, blue, red, purple, orange, step up, step down, swan-shaped basket, wait, is that a duck? Shit, calm down, calm down...

She shut her eyes again once they all stepped in and the old man secured the basket shut. She felt Brody and Jay close in on her, their body heat slightly brushing away the terror beating through her chest. When she felt them lift, she focused on her breathing and the comfort of being surrounded by her men.

"Open your eyes, baby." Brody's voice was full of joy, giving Taylor the courage to slowly lift her eyelids. Her breath caught in the back of her throat at the divine bird's-eye view of Male Order.

"Do you like it?" Jay's excitement matched Brody's enthusiasm.

The night air softly kissed her face as she took in the glowing glitter of the town's night lights. Dark navy velvet sprinkled with millions of diamonds hovered above. Its beauty evaporated all fear.

Keeping her eyes on the scenery, she spoke to the men behind her. "I feel like I'm in Heaven every time I'm with you two. You make it seem like any troubles I have are insignificant to the happiness I feel when I'm standing here."

"If this is Heaven," Jay whispered in her ear, "then I'd gladly die again."

Taylor smiled at his declaration. "Wait," Taylor turned her attention to Brody, "so what's in your box then?"

Brody pulled out a long, large box and opened it toward him. It was pale lavender, Stephanie & Co.'s signature shade. "We thought you might like this for after the cotillion tomorrow night." Turning it toward her, Taylor gasped at the platinum vibrator encrusted with rubies and black diamonds.

"It's perfect!" she exclaimed as she eagerly grabbed it from its box.

"I put batteries in it before we came," Brody replied proudly. Taylor giggled at the annoyed eye roll he got out of Jay.

"Well," said Taylor as she seductively looked up at her men, "if it has its batteries, why wait for the cotillion?"

She watched their shocked faces as she zipped down the back of her dress and let it puddle to her stilettos. She stood in nothing but her black lace garter belt, fishnet stockings, and of course, her Louboutins. Her body-hugging dress hadn't allowed her to wear a bra or panties.

"I have a feeling we're going to have to get used to this position," replied Jay as he and Brody again fell to their knees.

"If this is what they call a ball and chain, then lock me up and throw away the key." Brody licked his lips, his eyes transfixed on the v between her legs as he crawled to her waiting pussy. Nothing made her drip more than the sight of Brody and Jay at her feet, two of the world's richest and most dashing men, aching to lick and suck her into paradise.

She gripped the sides of the basket and let her head fall back, relishing the twirling movements of two wet tongues lavishing her pussy with southern hospitality. She looked down in time to see Brody turn on her new vibrator and press it against her swollen clit, causing her body to jerk at the intensity of the toy.

"I want your cocks in my mouth," she panted out through her struggling breathing.

Smack!

Taylor flinched at the burning slap Jay's large hand made against her bare ass. "No woman of ours will ever put our sexual pleasure before her own."

The combination of the spanking and Jay's dominating tone pushed Taylor over the edge of her orgasmic cliff. She clenched their hair in both hands and moaned loudly as she rode out her climax.

Jay and Brody rose to their feet and began to help her back in her dress, gingerly running their hands across her curves as they zipped her back in. The post-orgasm brain fog had yet to recede when they were lowered to the ground. She went up as a frightened girl and came back down as a fearless woman. She felt like a million bucks. Wait, make that a billion.

Chapter 13

Orders were barked, fashion interns were crying, the caterers were making their rounds with the fresh mimosas and shrimp hors d'oeuvres, yet amongst all the chaos, Taylor's world moved slowly and soundlessly around her.

Even with her Dallas debutante/pageant queen lifestyle, she had never experienced the riches of life until now. She had two painfully beautiful billionaires standing at the back of the room while they got their measurements taken for the exclusive designer shirts. She watched as Jay and Brody ignored the fashion assistants tugging and pinning at them. It looked like Brody was telling Jay an extensive, funny story. He talked with his hands animatedly, his eyes wide then slits when he would laugh with Jay every minute or so. Jay stared straight at Brody, giving him a closed-lip smile and nodding as he listened intently. When they would laugh at the same time, Brody would grab Jay's forearm for a few seconds as if he sought balance as they both flung their heads back in laughter.

Taylor's chest tightened and her insides warmed as she watched her men together. The history between the two was always so obvious. As different as they were, anyone that knew them could feel the brotherhood between the young men. But it was most apparent, Taylor thought, when they laughed together. They shared the same sense of boyish humor, and they always laughed at the same things, quoted the same movies, and just simply got lost in their own world together. When Jay and Brody got into a conversation, it was like watching two kids in a tree house with nothing but their flashlights, comic books, and perverted jokes to keep them happy.

"Okay, muse, stand up straight." Jeremiah's orders brought Taylor's attention back to the art piece of a gown she was being fitted for. The gown was made of a dark crimson, almost burgundy, Bordeaux satin that brought out the soft gold of Taylor's sun-kissed skin. It was strapless with an asymmetrical neckline. The top half was designed with the material in diagonal pleats and ruching, and the bottom half draped like it was trained well. The corset-like design had her breasts kissing each other, the boning had her waist looking incredibly small, and the A-line silhouette exaggerated the feminine curves of her hips.

Some say to stand by the ocean to realize man's insignificance compared to the power of nature. Taylor decided one should have their own custom Jeremiah Giordano evening gown to know woman's insignificance compared to the power of fashion.

Jeremiah shooed away an intern with a swish of a small hand when the girl silently held up two different, but equally dazzling, jeweled necklaces. It was the young girl's sixth attempt at picking out a necklace to match Taylor's gown. And for the sixth time, she lowered her head, turned away, and walked back to the eight-foot-long table covered in hundreds of pieces of jewelry.

The men had wanted to buy Taylor her cotillion jewelry the day before, but she had explained to them she would have no idea what to choose until she saw Jeremiah's finished product. Jay and Brody felt the obvious solution to the problem was buying the entire, brand-spanking-new fall line at Stephanie's.

Not used to seeing so many diamonds, jewels, and precious metals all at once, she left the task to Jeremiah, who then left the task to the green coed who was again bent at the waist, her face inches from the jewelry as she carefully scanned each piece in search of the perfect complement to Jeremiah's wearable art.

"All right, honey bun. Let me help you out of the gown so I can quickly do the alterations before you're due out." Jeremiah moved behind her and unzipped her dress carefully as four other assistants held the gown up so Taylor could step out without causing a wrinkle to the fine piece.

Taylor crossed her arms across her chest, suddenly aware she was standing on a platform surrounded by dozens of people, though they all seemed too preoccupied to notice Taylor's lingerie-clad body. She felt a little chilly, wearing little to nothing in a black lace-up corset and a black thong only slightly covered by a garter belt that held up her thin fishnets. And yet another pair of new stilettos. This time, she'd chosen Manolos.

"Are you cold, princess?" Jay's husky voice trailed down the back of her neck, sending shivers down her spine as he rested his large hands on her hips. Taylor leaned back against his chest, allowing him to wrap his arms around her shivering body. It was like he was her own personal Snuggie, and the chill began to recede.

"Okay, people, everyone's on break!" Brody started to herd the crowd out the double doors. "C'mon now, everyone. Be back in half an hour. Go, go, go!"

Brody shut the door behind the last person that scattered out, then he turned to Taylor with a devilish grin curling his lips up. "You really can't expect to wear something like that in front of us and not get fucked."

* * * *

Cinderella whimpered two soft squeals in the passenger seat, softly placing her cherry-manicured paw on Amber's thigh in desperation for her attention. She was wearing the new open-toe doggy stilettos Amber bought to match hers for last week's summer pool bash at the W-Dallas Victory Hotel. Amber knew that was Cinderella's way of letting her know she needed to relieve herself, but the hairball of a burden would have to wait.

"Enough of the dramatics, you little brat!" Amber yelled when the tiny dog's pleas grew more insistent. "Keep up that whining, and no sushi for a week." As if Cinderella understood the words, she lowered her head with her ears laid back and cowered back into the seat. Amber always knew to use the s-word when she needed Cinderella to shut the hell up. The little accessory would do anything for her sushi.

"Mama is trying to find a very bad lady, and you're doing *nothing but distracting me*!" The increase in her voice must have been a bit too much of intimidation because suddenly Cinderella began to shake and pee on the leather interior of the passenger seat.

"Goddamn it! Stupid little rat!"

Cinderella scurried to the back of the car, out of reach from the oncoming fury of Amber's fist.

"Go ahead and hide, you fucking useless fleabag. Once we get back home, I'm trading you in for a Pomeranian. Poodles are so last fall anyway!"

Amber's anger morphed into relief when she spotted two German shepherds sniffing around a corner store up ahead. It was an easy, quick, and convenient solution to the pink rat in the backseat that was only slowing Amber down.

Almost as if she sensed Amber's devious plan, Cinderella began to whimper again.

"Oh, it'll only hurt for a second, I'm sure," Amber replied coldly. She pulled into the store parking lot and looked around. She saw no sign of an owner for the two abandoned tramps. Before Cinderella had a chance to get away, Amber grabbed her by her pearl collar and threw her over to the two large dogs.

Amber pressed her foot to the pedal and sped off. She saw the faint trace of terror in Cinderella's eyes when she looked in her review mirror and saw the two snarling dogs slowly stalk and approach the tiny poodle with hunger in their eyes.

Amber ignored the devastated fading whimpers coming from Cinderella, concentrating on the directions coming from her GPS. She had been driving for half an hour, and even with the top down, the Texas heat was causing her to layer her powder foundation on her face thicker to cover the sweat streaks made through the makeup. The gel that smoothed down her platinum extensions was beginning to wear off, causing her hair to turn into a frizzy mess. She needed a mirror stat.

Amber stopped at a small, indiscreet motel to quickly change before her search for Brody's home. She pulled her hair back into a chignon finished with the rest of her can of Aqua Net, added another layer of makeup, pulled on her zebra-print formal gown with side cutouts, strapped on her hot pink sequin heels, then took one last look in the mirror. *Goddamn, I'm a fine sonuvubitch…*

She smiled as she passed a sign that read *Male Order, Texas…The Lone Star's Favorite Mistake.*

Amber knew gaining access into the Bartlett estate would be near impossible with the security they would obviously have. She couldn't ask her useless, greedy father to put her on the list of allowed guests, so she went to his longtime assistant, Alvin Pratt.

Alvin had been molesting Amber with his eyes since she was just a girl with a training bra and braces, so yesterday she took full advantage of Chester Molester's pedophilic fantasies. Knowing Alvin was working alone in his office late last night, Amber strolled in dressed in her old high school cheerleader uniform, dropped to her knees behind his desk, and sucked his tiny prick until his balls were drained dry.

By the time she woke up in her bed this morning, she'd received a text from Alvin assuring she will be on the list of guests for the Bartlett's pre-cotillion party. Not bad for a mere forty seconds of work.

It didn't take her long to find Brody's house. It trumped any mansion she or her friends had ever been in, much less lived in.

A flame of jealousy shot through her at the thought of Taylor being lucky to bag Brody Bartlett, the Texas Prince William. The bitch was always so damn lucky. Anything Amber wanted, Taylor got. Amber wanted to be the beauty queen of Dallas, Taylor got it.

Amber wanted to be a local icon, Taylor got it. Amber wanted a rock star boyfriend, Taylor got it. Amber wanted a beautiful billionaire prince, and guess what? Taylor got it. But it was all about to come to an epic end.

Security gave her no trouble when they confirmed she was a guest on the list.

As Amber made her way up the winding driveway, she was happy to see how easy it was to go unnoticed. There were hundreds of cars scattered everywhere. There were people everywhere, as well. One large group, consisting of several high-fashion assistants to God-knows-who, was pulling out formal wear, sewing machines, and yards of material. A group of caterers and bartenders pulled out trays of food and catering equipment.

According to Amber's father, family members, friends, and business partners of the Bartletts would fly in from around the world to lodge at the Bartlett estate every year for the town's annual cotillion. It would be held tonight, and it looked like the pre-party was already in full swing.

The most elite of the south walked around the property, chatting joyously as the held their jeweled masks in front of their eyes. Amber felt a rare pang of insecurity course through her as she watched a crowd of gorgeous young women dressed in royal, custom-designed ball gowns giggle past an even bigger group of even more gorgeous men. The men bowed their heads in polite admiration while the women waved and blew kisses.

Amber parked her car next to the others and stuffed the micro camcorder in her bra. She hurried out of the car and walked through the quickly growing crowd of help and guests, careful to keep her mask in front of her eyes in case she prematurely ran into Miss Shit Don't Stink.

Walking down the halls of the gorgeous mansion, she looked in each room as she passed the open doors. Each held different women being fitted into extravagant designer gowns. More fury burned in Amber's face.

Bingo! Right there, in a room at least five times larger than the others she passed, was Taylor Ewing, surrounded by a glam team of makeup artists, hair stylists, and several seamstresses as she stood on a platform in front of a three-way mirror. Behind Taylor stood the hunky Brody, along with another gorgeous beefcake, as they stared at Taylor like she was Playmate of the fucking Century.

Wait! Is that Jeremiah Giordano!

Just as the famous designer began to help Taylor out of her dress, revealing that damn body that stole Amber's crowns so many times, a black-clad female assistant with blood red lips, white skin, and a bob haircut came over and closed the double doors with a big thud that echoed through the high walls.

"Damn it!" Amber cursed under her breath as she leaned on the wall by the doors. But just a minute later, the doors opened, and the herd of help scattered out. Amber turned her head to get a peek of why everyone was leaving, but that same black-clad assistant once again closed the doors before she could look.

"What the fuck, bitch?" Amber didn't give a shit if she was supposed to be blending into the uptight crowd of idiots. This was getting annoying and frustrating.

The petite assistant cocked a brow and peered over her artsy black-rimmed glasses. "Look, *beetch*," she began in a heavy French accent, "Mr. Bartlett and Mr. Stephens need some time to talk to their new girlfriend. Now if you had any sort of brain underneath that horse hair—"

"Wait!" Amber interrupted, uncharacteristically ignoring the insult. "Girlfriend? Did you say *their* girlfriend? Taylor Ewing is fucking two men!"

The assistant gave her a puzzling look. "But you are in *Male Order,* mademoiselle." Then she walked off, shaking her head and mumbling in French.

A smile spread wide on Amber's face when she almost immediately began to hear a soft, feminine panting coming through the doors. Amber looked around to make sure no one was looking, then she dropped to her knees and peered through the keyhole.

Holy shit! This was a better surprise than when she babysat for her father's pro-golf buddy. Instead of walking in to find his two children playing in the house, the golfer had been sprawled out on the couch, naked with nothing but a huge red bow covering his cock. That night she left with two grand. It was still one of her finest accomplishments. Until now…

Brody already had Taylor's tits in his mouth, and the other man had his head buried between her thighs. Amber quickly fumbled with her padded bra to reach for the micro camera. Then she gingerly placed the lens in the keyhole.

Amber grabbed her cell phone from her pocket and scrolled down her contact list to the E's.

"*Hola*? Amber?" Emilio sounded eager on the other line.

"Get ready to thank me, Emilio. You're about to become a real star."

"You got them on tape?"

"Oh, I got something better than that. Try Brody and his buddy making themselves a little Taylor sandwich! And get this, she's committed to *both* of them!"

Emilio gasped. "*Aye, mira que* wow! Double the trouble! Good job, *mija*. Give me thirty minutes, and I'll be on my way."

Amber flipped her phone closed and waited patiently for her plan to come to fruition.

Chapter 14

Jeremiah wasn't too happy with his "muse", as he'd called Taylor since they met the day before. When the staff's half-hour break expired, Jeremiah walked through the doors and screeched in terror at the disheveled pile of hay that had once been Taylor's updo, and then he covered his mouth in horror at the tiny, black mascara trails that ran down her cheeks from crying out in tortuous pleasure.

Jeremiah pushed Taylor back down in the salon chair a little too roughly.

"Hey!" she scolded her new friend. "Keep the butch love taps to a minimum, ok?"

Jeremiah stood next to her reflection as the glam squad quickly went back to work to repair Taylor's sex aftermath. He sure looked pissed, standing there with his fists on his narrow little hips, his glossed lips in a thin line of scorn. "Muse, I have a Y-chromosome and an unarguable plethora of male models begging for my sweet little mouth, and I still don't understand your insatiable need for a good fuck every damn hour."

Taylor's head was being jerked in all directions, hands brushing and curling and spraying in a deep panic, but she remained calm and kept her eyes on Jeremiah's animated mannerisms. "Look at them, Jeremiah," Taylor stated flatly. "How insatiable would *you* be?"

Jeremiah sucked his teeth and raised his chin in the mirror reflection, crossing his arms as he let out a defeated sigh. "Touché, my muse."

Taylor stared back at Jeremiah with a smile, satisfied she had made her point.

* * * *

Jeremiah's glam squad had worked their magic in less than fifteen minutes. Looking perfectly polished, no one would ever guess Taylor had just been taken by two men at the same time not even a half hour ago.

After giving her sincere thanks to the staff that helped create her fairy tale ending, she looped her arms through each of the men's biceps as they stood on either side of her. They looked so dashing in their Tom Ford formal wear. Jay had chosen black on black, and Brody opted for a white shirt under his black vest with a skinny black tie hanging fashionably messy.

As they strolled happily out of Brody's mansion, they were met by a round, two-horse drawn carriage. "Is this our ride?" Taylor's life with Brody and Jay was already getting better and better. "Now I *really* feel like a princess." It was gorgeous. Made of white iron, vines of lilies and roses snaked through the metal work.

"It's yours," Brody said softly in her ear.

Did she just hear him right? "*Mine*? You bought me a carriage?"

"We didn't buy it. We had it made for you," Brody corrected. "Well, *I* had it made for you. Jay was still being a little bitch about you at the time." That gained Brody a growl of warning from Jay, but Brody just continued as his deep, chocolate eyes seared into hers. "After that first time we met you in Veronica's yard, I immediately knew you would be our date to the cotillion. So I had this carriage made."

"I don't understand. What made you feel the need to buy me this when you had only planned on asking me on a date?"

"First of all," Jay lifted her chin so she diverted her attention away from the pair of puppy dog eyes to Jay's shimmering jade irises, "no woman of ours will ever be denied feeling anything less than the princess she is. And now that you're ours, this will be your ride every time we have a ball to attend. We want the whole world to know our Sleeping Beauty is now awake."

Taylor couldn't help but swoon at Jay's declaration. It had been the sweetest thing Jay had ever said to her, and it melted her heart.

* * * *

The cotillion made any pretentious gala in Dallas look like a hoedown. They passed through the giant solid-gold doors and into a paradise of Male Order royalty, the divine music of a live orchestra, and, most importantly, an abundance of the finest food.

The wealthy guests wore the finest furs, the rarest diamonds, and the latest designs. They danced to the music of the large orchestra, which Taylor found out had flown from across the world to come to perform at this cotillion. She recognized several famous politicians and celebrities, all of whom looked at home within the Male Order crowd.

Taylor spent most of her time with Brody's and Jay's mothers who insisted she meet every single person they knew. She had been most excited to finally meet Brody's fathers. They'd just arrived from London the night before, and they seemed beyond thrilled to find out their son was in love.

She was having a conversation with Greta about starting private yoga lessons next week when she felt a large hand on her shoulder. She turned to see Brody and Jay grinning wide at her.

"Excuse me, Mrs. McCall. We're going to take a little walk with our Taylor," said Brody as he grabbed her hand.

"Right now? But we might miss the bachelor auction." Both men cocked up an eyebrow at her. "I mean, not that it concerns me or anything." She attempted her best good-girl smile and allowed them to escort her out.

"What is this all about?" asked Taylor once they'd stepped outside. They were leading her to the side of the building.

"Remember when we told you about the day in economics when Brody and I decided to build our own empire? Well, after class that day, we had come by here to make that wish official." They stopped in front of an old-fashioned water well that stood alone in the open grass. Jay held out a quarter for her to take. "It's never let us down, and it'll do the same for you."

Taylor smiled at them. They never stopped putting effort into being romantic, and she felt special they felt they could share so much with her.

"Kiss for good luck?" She held the coin out for each man to kiss before she kissed them both. She closed her eyes and held the coin tightly in her grip as she concentrated on her wish, then she threw it in the well. She turned back to them. "Now we'll see if it comes true. Come on, let's go back inside. My champagne glass is almost empty."

She began to pull them along, but they both stood still. "What's wrong?"

"I heard the coin drop in the bucket," replied Jay with a slight grin. "It has to drop in the water to count."

"I heard it, too," Brody agreed as he nodded.

"You're being silly. I've never heard of that. We'll do it again later. I really want to go back and dance more."

Jay shrugged. "It won't work if you wait. Guess you'll have to do it again."

"Fine," Taylor complied as she pulled on the rope hanging through the well. When the bucket came in sight, she reached in and felt around for the coin. She gasped when she felt a small velvet box and yanked it out as quickly as she could.

"Omigod, omigod, omigod!" she rambled in excitement. She ripped the bow off and opened the box, revealing the hugest blue diamond ring she had ever seen. On either side lay two pear-cut white diamonds. She about fainted when she quickly estimated it to be at least ten carats.

"Taylor Marie Ewing, will you be our bride?" She looked up from the ring when she heard their voices. They both knelt on one knee. She could barely make out their hopeful looks as she struggled to keep her tears from falling too rapidly.

She looked from Brody to Jay. "Say you'll marry us, princess," Jay said when she didn't speak. Between the cotillion, the two gorgeous billionaires on their knees before her, and the twenty-million dollar engagement ring just seconds from being hers, her mind struggled to make sense of the overwhelming situation. She kept running Brody's and Jay's words through her mind several times before they registered.

"Yes."

"Yes?" Both men looked at each other with excitement in their eyes.

"Yes! Yes, of course I'll marry you both."

The three embraced as they stood in the Texas night. Jay pulled the extravagant ring from the box and placed it on Taylor's left ring finger. The more she looked at it, the more it took her breath away.

Brody grabbed her face back and brushed her lips with the pad of his thumb as he stared at them with hunger in his eyes. "You had sealed your fate as our bride-to-be the moment I laid eyes on this angel face. Just about the prettiest thing I ever saw."

Taylor felt Jay's hands tighten around her waist as he moved behind her, his long erection prodding the back of her dress, and then she parted her mouth for Brody's kiss, needing to feel their warm, hard bodies against her just one more time before they went to the ball.

But the kiss was interrupted by the slow, loud, mocking clapping of a single pair of hands. "Bravo! Bravo! Y'all are a regular Romeo and Juliet, only Juliet's fucking Mercutio, too!"

Horror flooded through Taylor's body when her eyes came upon Amber standing right in front of them on the lawn. Taylor could feel her hands start to shake against Brody's chest. The men looked confused, but they came in closer in protection.

Amber contorted her face into a faux look of surprise. "I'm sorry, B.F.F. Did I get the story wrong? Hmm." Amber held a finger to her mouth as she looked back and forth between Jay and Brody, emphasizing her mock pondering. "Now which one is the werewolf and which is the vampire? No, no, y'all are much, much too finely built to be a couple of pussy-whipped little boys. Ooh! I know!" Amber clapped once again, the loud sound causing the terrified Taylor to flinch. "Mr. Big and Aidan! The American iconic balance of an alpha dick and a beta pussy. Yes, that's *much* more suitable." Amber's eyes were now stone-cold and glaring straight at Taylor.

"Excuse me, ma'am, but this is private property."

"I suggest you see yourself off the premises before we put you out," Jay remarked after Brody.

"Ooh, all this manly hostility is giving me a wettie."

"What are you doing here, Amber?" Taylor felt like she was going to be sick. She'd known Amber long enough to know that glare was the kiss of death. Taylor didn't know what Amber was up to, but she did know the pampered brat was never up to any good when she wore that expression. Taylor was afraid, and anyone who knew Amber personally would testify that she had every reason to be.

"Amber?" Brody's blazed with rage as realization must have dawned on him. Taylor had told them about that fateful night at Dillon's apartment. "Get the fuck out of here."

"Oh, of course. Please, do allow me, good gentleman." Amber curtsied and bowed her head as a menacing giggle escaped her lips. "But, there is one thing I forgot to mention."

Taylor closed her eyes as she waited for the black widow to inject her poison into Taylor's fairy tale.

"I just so happen to now be the proud owner of a sex tape showing the two of you aboard the Ewing Express. *Choo-choo!*" Amber made a motion like she was pulling on an invisible horn string.

"Oh God, no." Taylor struggled to swallow the hot tears that pricked at her eyes.

"You see, this here," Amber pulled out a small, white device from her triple-padded bra, "is a state-of-the-art micro camcorder. Very good picture, I'd say." Amber's eyes danced with joy as if she relished the pain that radiated from Taylor's heart. "Maybe if you weren't such a horny slut, it would have been a little harder for my plan to work out. But lucky me, you didn't waste a moment of time once you were alone with these two." Amber gave both men a slow onceover before perversely licking her injected lips with her tongue. "Not that I could blame you, B.F.F."

"Brody, get security over to get this psycho out of my sight." Jay's voice was full of anger and annoyance.

"Don't move a step until I'm done," Amber ordered ferociously.

"Why are you doing this, Amber?" Taylor cursed the shaking in her voice, but it was taking everything she had to not have a full-on anxiety attack.

"Why?" Amber laughed as if the answer was so obvious. "What do you mean why? Because you're a snotty little bitch who thinks she's too good for anyone that doesn't live up to your pathetic Mother Teresa image."

No matter what, Taylor had once cared deeply for Amber, and the words hurt. She chocked back a small sob. "You know me, Amber. And you know that's not true. Maybe you were only out for the title and crown, but you *know* my heart belonged to my charity work."

"Then join the fucking Peace Corps! Become a nun, become a nurse, become a dick-sucker working pro bono for all I give a shit!" Amber's face was a tomato-red, deepening in color as her voice raised in volume. "Everything was perfect until you and your white-trash mama decided to trample into Dallas high-society like a couple of fucking hippos!"

Like a light switch, Taylor's emotions went from distraught to furious. Mama insults weren't taken lightly by any southerner. "Keep my mama out of your cum-coated mouth, Amber. I'm warning you!" Taylor had never spoken to Amber that way, but the woman was losing her mind before her very eyes.

"And what the fuck are you going to do about it, Taylor? It's over. You can kiss the Miss Dallas Texas Yellow Rose crown buh-bye. And once your charity gets word about this, you'll never work for another organization ever again. Sick people just don't like whores, Taylor. But I'm not one to gossip, so you didn't hear it from me."

"You evil bitch." Taylor gritted her teeth as red flooded her vision.

"Well, I prefer demonic, but evil does the job, I suppose." Amber gave her a teasing wink. That's all it took to blow Taylor's fuse. She lunged for the heartless heifer, but Brody caught her by one arm, holding her firmly by his side.

"You're one dumb bitch if you think we're going to let you leave with that camera." Jay began to step forward but stopped when they all noticed a white Jeep making its way down the winding driveway.

You've got to be kidding me.

"And here's my accomplice now." Amber's heavily lined lips radiated pride through a toothy, veneered grin.

The white Jeep came to a sudden stop beside Amber and out bounced a cheerful Emilio Estefan, pretty much the last person on Earth you want around your leaked sex tape.

"How the hell did he get past security?" asked Brody in frustration.

"It's Emilio Estefan," Taylor replied. "He gets what he wants, where he wants, as quick as he wants, and you'll never find out his sources. He's like a phantom rolled in sequins."

"Why *hello,* gentleman!" exclaimed Emilio as he peered over his heart-shaped sunglasses, despite it being nighttime. "Mmm, the girl does have good taste, if you ask me." Emilio turned his attention to Amber, his tone turning serious. "Did you get it?" Taylor watched defenselessly as Amber tossed the tiny camera into Emilio's small brown hands.

"This isn't happening! This isn't happening!" Taylor sobbed against Jay's chest as panic flooded her body. Everything she'd worked for since she was a twelve-year-old child would become irrelevant by tonight. All the people she helped, all the money she raised, all the years she devoted would be a distant memory. She wouldn't even have to wait for press time. Emilio had the most popular gossip blog in the Lone Star state, and that meant the video would immediately be spread throughout the internet in a matter of minutes.

Amber wiped imaginary dirt off her hands and onto her gown. "Well, looks like our work here is done, Emilio. What do you say we go back into town and grab a drink at Let Them Eat Beefcake? First lap dance is on me."

"I don't think I'll be joining you tonight, Amber." An odd smile rested on Emilio's lips, and Taylor noticed he had yet to take his eyes off her.

"Don't be a fag, Emilio. This is the best day of my life, and all I want right now is an ice-cold martini in my right hand and a throbbing stripper dick in the other. Now move it, Emilio! Or did you forget how to walk after a long night of ass pounding?" Emilio just continued to stare at Taylor with a knowing grin.

Amber's frustration spilled through her voice when Emilio didn't move an inch. "Why the fuck are you just standing there? Get your queer ass in the damn car, now!"

"Oh, but *mijita*, just because you're done doesn't mean I am."

Taylor stared back into Emilio's laughing hazel eyes, and the wave of panic returned. *God help me, he has more!*

The group didn't keep their eyes off of Emilio as he reached in his car and pulled out a brown paper-wrapped package held neatly together with a simple piece of twine.

"You see, Taylor," Emilio casually tossed the package from one delicate hand to the other, "I've had my eye on you for a very long time." He turned his knowing smile to Amber. "You, too, Ambueler. Or do you prefer Miss Teen Dallas Texas Cowgirl Spur?"

With the power of a freight train, realization dawned upon Taylor the instant Emilio mentioned Amber's old title.

"What the fuck has gotten into you? And why the hell are you calling me that? I was like thirteen when I was Miss Teen Dallas Texas Cowgirl Spur." Apparently, Amber was a little slower at catching on.

Emilio dropped his head back in laughter at Amber's ignorance. "Oh, Amber, Amber, Amber. I'm guessing none of the wolves that raised you taught you the virtue of karma." He fiddled with his bangles, and that's when Taylor noticed for the first time that Emilio wore one of her charity's rubber red HCM-awareness bracelets. "I mean, *I* say blame the parents, but too bad the stars don't take poor upbringing into consideration."

"What's with the psycho babbling bullshit? Can you tell me what the hell you're talking about?" Taylor could hear fear in Amber's voice. She was getting scared of what Emilio had up his sleeve.

"You're the little boy from the charity ball," Taylor pointed out. "I remember your honey-colored eyes and how your brown skin brought out their color. Amber and I were about thirteen, and you asked us for an autograph. I could never forget how sweet you had been to us."

Emilio's smile faded as the memory rushed in. "Yes, I was a very sick child at the time. It took all the strength I had to get up that morning, but I remember how excited I was to meet you two. I was utterly captivated by your beauty, and I admired the devotion you had to making others like me feel better." Emilio bit down on his bottom lip as it began to tremble. "Two real princesses, right there in front of me. When you spoke to me, Taylor, your face was so full of caring, and you looked me right in the eye even though I looked like I was near death. I had never felt so *visible* in my life as I did when you knelt down to my level to talk to me. It was like I was the only person you were able to see in the entire room."

Tears flowed down Emilio's face as he turned to Amber. Taylor noticed that Amber's face had grown pale and clammy, and Taylor guessed the memory was finally starting to come back to her. "But you, Amber, killed a small part of that child that night. You killed the trust and optimism every untainted child carries with them. I learned that day that even the most beautiful of roses carry sharp thorns, ready to draw blood from any *tonto* hypnotized with their phony image.

"After spending days in bed crying, I got over it. I learned that day there was something called a bad person. I vowed to become a pioneer for the truth. The public wants to know who the real ungrateful little shits are, the assholes that live lies, fooling others into believing they are good people, normal people, when they're only snakes in the grass." Emilio stood in front of Amber to look her in her wide, terrified eyes. Taylor had never even heard of anyone ever putting Amber Fox in her place.

Emilio held up the brown package in front of Amber's face. "This package, *aqui,* holds hundreds of candid photos from the last several years. These are unreleased photos that no one has ever seen. Each one is of you in a compromising position with several very powerful men that would not be happy to hear about the leaking of these photos. I can't decide which one is more scandalous, the one with the congressman on his knees in front of you while y'all hide in an alley, the one of you riding a Heisman winner in his truck while his pregnant wife hosts her baby shower at home, or maybe the one of you and Mrs.—"

"Stop it!" Amber covered her ears with her hands, her face streaked with black rivers of running mascara. She sobbed in her hands while the group watched in silence.

"Look at me, Amber," Emilio whispered softly. Amber's puffy red eyes looked up at the young man, snot dripping and pooling in the crease of her mouth. Emilio held her face gently with his hands, and he gingerly brushed aside a few stray hairs hanging in her face. "Now I want you to look at me when I say this." Amber nodded, her breathing still heavy. "*I* did this to you, Amber. *I'm* the one." Emilio's voice could barely be made out through the whisper, but the venom on his tongue was sharp as a knife. "From this day on, you will be forced to face the person you truly are. And when you do, I want you to remember me. My fans want the truth, and *I'm* the one that gives it to them. Me, Amber, the dying freak, and I never want you to forget that."

Amber stood motionless from shock as Emilio turned to face the trio.

Just then, a Male Order police car slowly pulled up in front of the building. Two officers approached the group, both sexy brunets, only one looked to be in his early thirties, maybe ten years younger than his partner. Their expressions were serious and firm although their sexuality was no less hidden.

"Ma'am," the older of the two addressed Amber, "is that your pink BMW in the lot?"

Amber didn't answer, only stood still as a statue, her empty eyes fixed on an unknown point beyond them.

"This is her vehicle, Officer Jones," Brody answered when Amber didn't. "And I would like her to be escorted off our premises, or I will need to file a trespassing charge on this…*disturbed* young lady."

"Well, we're already about to arrest her for unreasonable abandonment of an animal and attempting to cause two animals to fight another," the younger one informed them.

Jay walked toward Amber, grabbed the keys to the pink Beamer from the psycho's limp hand, and handed them to the officer. "This is her vehicle, Officer Stabler. Here are her keys."

Officer Stabler's words suddenly registered, and panic rose in Taylor's chest. "Cinderella! What happened? Is everything okay?"

"We saw this woman throw her small dog like a grade-A rib eye toward our K-9s, Edward and Eric, then watched from a distance as she peeled out of the gas station like a bat out of hell, obviously trying to get our dogs to kill the defenseless creature." Officer Jones threw a disgusted look at Amber.

Taylor could hardly believe what she heard. Taylor knew Amber was not the ideal pet owner, often teasing Cinderella with sushi and wonton crisps and forcing her to wear tacky outfits that matched her own, but she never imagined Amber could be capable of such cruelty. Then again, Amber's parents had a house staff that ensured the family pets were all well taken care of.

Taylor thought of the dozens of times she pet-sat the tiny cherub so that Amber could go out on a hot date without the "burden" of her little dog. In all the time Taylor had spent with Cinderella, she had yet to recall any burdens the obedient little thing brought. Taylor enjoyed their sushi and reality show nights together while they lounged in their pink Snuggies.

Just then, Cinderella came running out of the police car, followed by two large German shepherds. The tiny dog jumped in Taylor's outstretched arms, her tail wagging enthusiastically to indicate how happy she was to see her.

Taylor was still comforting the neglected animal when Amber's sudden voice broke in.

"She's a whiney little shit." Amber's eyes were still emotionless as she continued to stare off into the distance. "And she eats all my sushi."

Officer Jones looked at Amber like she had just said she ate shit for breakfast. "Your *sushi*? Like, raw fish sushi?" He sounded more disgusted at the thought than weirded out by the random remark.

Amber blinked in puzzlement. "The nasty slut was always jealous of my shoe collection, so she needed to die."

Cinderella shook when Amber talked. The poodle whimpered softly at the insult as she nuzzled Taylor's neck with her little wet nose. "It's okay, Cinda-Relly. You'll never have to beg for sushi again. We're going to take good care of you. And we're trading in these cheap clothes of yours with some couture." Taylor thought about the doggie boutique, Doggy Style, on the square. They would go shopping for a new wardrobe in the morning, and those excruciating-looking stilettos on Cinda-Relly's tiny paws would be the first to go.

Officer Jones let out a frustrated sigh and looked up at the sky while he shook his head. "So it's one of those days," he said to Officer Stabler under his breath as he ran his fingers through his salt-and-pepper hair.

"Okay, ma'am," Officer Stabler turned Amber around and snapped on the cuffs, "you have the right to remain silent. Anything you say can and will be held against you in a court of law…"

Taylor, Brody, Jay, and Emilio watched the police car drive down the long driveway with the beauty-queen-turned-animal-abuser hunched over in the backseat.

"Looks like y'all won't have to worry about her coming back anytime soon," Emilio announced triumphantly. "And if she does, you have more than enough leverage for a lifetime in this." He indicated the brown package still gripped in his hands. "Hey, *papi chulo*, catch!" Emilio called out to Jay as he threw the heavy package at him.

"Oomph!" Jay's large frame bent forward from the force of the package ramming into his gut. Looking slightly embarrassed, Jay straightened and cleared his throat. "Nice arm you got there, brother."

"You should hear what they say about my *third* arm." Emilio laughed then reached in his pocket and tossed the mini camcorder to Brody. "I wish y'all the best of luck. You especially deserve it, Taylor. You'll be the prettiest princess bride since Grace Kelly." Emilio winked, and Taylor smiled her appreciation through tears of joy and shock of all that happened in the last twenty minutes. "See you soon, my living princess." Taylor watched as her fairy godmother skipped to his Jeep, then rode off into the Texas night.

Chapter 15

Eight weeks later

Mrs. Stephens-Bartlett couldn't get over how much leg room she had in their new executive jet. And she couldn't stop staring at the diamond-encrusted white dress that hung just a few feet away from her. It was almost a shame Jeremiah had gone through all that trouble for her to just wear it once.

Maybe one day I'll have my own little princess to hand it down to.

Taylor smiled at the brief thought then leaned back in her seat with Cinderella sleeping soundly in her lap. She admired her wedding band, a circle of infinite diamonds. She moaned softly while Brody and Jay each massaged a sore foot that ached from dancing.

They'd had the night of their life the evening before, their wedding night. Six weeks ago, Brody and Jay had surprised Taylor with an engagement present. After two weeks of Taylor's whining about not being able to find a venue with enough room to pull off her dream wedding, the men did what they did best. They simply bought her one.

Her jaw was on the floor for a good hour after they had announced they bought her a private island in Brazil, complete with four houses, four beaches, and its own mini airport. The men named it *Ilha de Três*. They assured Taylor that at "only" two million dollars, the purchase had been a steal.

But *Ilha de Três* was a true paradise. It was the perfect spot to throw a party for their four hundred closest friends and family members. The babies ran around naked on the sand, old couples made new memories as they walked on the beach, young couples fell in love all over again as they swayed in the dozens of hammocks scattered throughout the island, and Cinderella surprised everyone by catching two small fish with her teeth as she waded on the shoreline. It was truly Heaven on Earth.

"Baby, look out the window." Jay's silky voice held a hint of eagerness.

Not opening her eyes, Taylor asked, "Are we there yet?"

"Yeah, darlin'. We're here," Brody confirmed. The newlyweds had planned a month-long honeymoon in Tuscany. Taylor was thrilled at the thought of spending a month in a little Tuscan hut while she and her gorgeous grooms relaxed with all the fresh pasta and rare wine they could ever want.

"Can you see our hut from here?" Taylor asked as she made her way to the window where the men looked out.

"Yeah, I guess you can say that," Brody replied with a smile.

The odd answer perked Taylor's curiosity as she scanned the landscape for the small stone hut. The jet was fairly low, but the little boxes below still seemed to just run together. "There's so many!" She turned to Brody and Jay. "Y'all said we could see it from here, but that's impossible." Both men only smiled in response.

She knew her men well enough by now to know when they were up to something. She cocked a brow and crossed her arms in front of her chest. "Okay, boys, spit it out! And don't tell me y'all made reservations at some chain resort. Y'all promised a real Tuscan experience for my wedding gift."

The boys laughed at the disappointed look that she was sure she wore by now. Sure, Taylor, like most girls, loved to be wined and dined. But it was the deep history and classic architecture that had made her choose Tuscany. Taylor valued history and foreign travel, and she felt that to experience either was a mind-expanding exercise.

She was really looking forward to a simple, authentic experience of temporarily living in a modest hut on the Tuscan water. No butlers, no cooks, no maids. Just Taylor taking care of her men, and her men taking care of her. If she wanted a materialistic honeymoon, she would have agreed to Dubai instead.

"No, princess, we're not going to a resort," Jay assured her. "Come here, sit on my lap, and I want you to look where I am pointing."

"I don't see anything."

"Look for the house with the red flag."

"But the only red flag is on that…" Taylor cupped a hand over her gaping mouth before she could finish her sentence.

"Castle?" Brody finished for her.

"Clutch the pearls," Taylor whispered as her hand lowered to her frantically beating heart.

"Pearls? You want pearls? There's an antique shop in town. We can head straight over there right after we unpack," Brody rambled, obviously jumping at any excuse to spoil her further.

Taylor attempted to shake a little of the shock from her head. "Um, no. No, honey, it was an expression. Aurora says it all the time…" Even as she spoke, she couldn't snap herself out of the gravitating pull of the magnificent castle that waited for her. *Her* castle, a *real* castle!

As ecstatic as she was at the thought, she couldn't fight the twinge of guilt in her gut. Taylor guessed the land had to range at least fifty acres, and the castle itself looked like it was built at least fifteen hundred years ago!

"Oh, Jay and Brody, I kind of feel guilty accepting—" Before she could blink, let alone finish her damn sentence, Taylor was sprawled out on Jay's lap with her ass high in the air. Moving just as quickly, she felt Brody lift her sundress and effortlessly rip her thong from her body. Before she could protest, she felt six hard slaps coming down on her bare ass. She whimpered loudly as the pain warmed her pussy, leaving a damp spot on Jay's knee. The enormous erection poking at her side did nothing to tame her dripping juices, either.

Jay bent his head down to whisper in her ear. "It pissed me off enough when you tried to stop me from spoiling you as your boyfriend, but now that I'm your husband, I'm completely offended."

Taylor breath caught in the back of her throat as she wondered what punishments lay ahead. "I'm sorry, Jay. I'll never question you again."

Jay nuzzled her hair with his nose, and he gently rubbed her tender ass cheeks. "That's my girl."

"I dunno, Jay. I think we ought to punish her good. Even princesses need to know their place in the presence of their kings."

Taylor looked over her shoulder to shoot Brody a glare. "You sure got a big mouth, Brody." He wiggled his eyebrows up and down at her, obviously enjoying the mischief he was creating.

"Hmm," Jay thought for a moment while Taylor held her breath in anticipation, "I think you might be right about this one, Brody. Grab that paddle we bought at Stephanie's before we left."

"Paddle?" Taylor panicked. No one had ever even spanked her before she met Jay and Brody, much less used a paddle on her. "Why can't you just use your hand?" Taylor loved the way Jay's large, masculine hands felt as they smacked sharp desire against her ass and, if she was being a *good* girl, her pussy.

"You just might like it," Brody said as Taylor looked up to see him pull a baby blue leather paddle with a solid gold handle out of a shopping bag. Taylor imagined the smooth texture of the leather slapping against her sensitive ass cheeks, and surprisingly, the thought made her wetter.

Brody turned back to Taylor. Looking down on her with a sly grin, he asked her in a low, seductive voice, "Are you ready for your something blue, Mrs. Stephens-Bartlett?"

Taylor stared back at the sparkle of devotion in Brody's eyes, and although Jay was supposed to be punishing her, he was casually running his fingers through her hair in affection.

Maybe one day, her husbands' gorgeous faces, sculpted bodies, impressive dicks, story-book romance gestures, extravagant gifts, and opulent lifestyle would grow old and boring. *Naah,* she thought with a smile as the cool, soft surface of the paddle came down on her impatient ass.

Epilogue

Mrs. Taylor Bartlett-Stephens: From the Lap of Luxury to the Arms of Luxury…

As you heard exclusively here on Allegedly last month, socialite and philanthropist Taylor Ewing *married The Velvet Rope founder* Brody Bartlett *complete with a civil union with co-founder* Jay Stephens. *The nuptials took place on a private Brazilian island Bartlett and Stephens bought for Ewing as an engagement present.*

After a four-week honeymoon in Tuscany (where the billionaire internet moguls bought their new bride a sixteen million dollar castle!), the newlyweds have since settled into a new mansion in Male Order, Texas, a small town right outside of Dallas.

Yesterday, Ewing announced on her Velvet Rope account that she is retiring from pageantry to devote more time to her foundation, Johnny Angel Foundation for Hypertrophic Cardiomyopathy Research, dedicated to her late father who passed away from the heart disease.

The same day the now ex-beauty queen posted the update, the trio was spotted with their adopted poodle, Cinderella. Ewing and the former sidekick and recovered victim of fallen pageant queen turned animal cruelty criminal Amber Fox *were seen having lunch in Austin at the Saltlick where they dined on barbecue and pecan pie.*

And looking at the paparazzo shots, either Taylor ate too much potato salad or someone is sporting a little baby bump! We later heard rumors of the trio shopping at a few baby boutiques on South Congress…Allegedly!

THE END

ABOUT THE AUTHOR

Lola grew up in small town Texas as the only girl in her family, thus harboring a healthy appetite for football and a great appreciation for the simple, rugged world of men. Her best friend describes her as "the guy's girl in lace," the one that can kick up her stilettos to enjoy a night of pigskin and Robert Rodriguez movies.

She is now a single mother working two jobs to support her childhood dream of being Meryl Streep in *She-Devil*.

Siren Publishing, Inc.
www.SirenPublishing.com

LaVergne, TN USA
02 February 2011
214921LV00010B/57/P